THE
PETER PAN
CHRONICLES

VOLUME 3
THE CALLALOO FICTION SERIES
Charles H. Rowell, Series Editor

THE PETER PAN CHRONICLES

CHARLES FRYE

UNIVERSITY PRESS OF VIRGINIA CHARLOTTESVILLE

ST. PHILIP'S COLLEGE LIBRARY

THE UNIVERSITY PRESS OF VIRGINIA
Copyright © 1989 by Charles Frye
First published 1989

Library of Congress Cataloging-in-Publication Data

Frye, Charles A.
    The Peter Pan Chronicles / Charles Frye.
       p.   cm. — (Callaloo fiction series ; v. 3)
    ISBN 0-8139-1223-7
    I. Title. II. Series.
   PS3556.R88P48 1989
   813'.54—dc19   88-35318
                                              CIP

Printed in the United States of America

FOR MY PARENTS AND THEIR GRANDCHILDREN

ACKNOWLEDGMENTS

Many thanks to Joyce Rose and Lorna Haines for their technical assistance in the preparation of the original manuscript and to Micheline Bousquet, Johnnella Butler, E. Ethelbert Miller, Janice Liddell, Rudine Sims, and Cynthia Packard, who read the early drafts and provided critical comments. Special thanks to Ken Blekicki, Theresa Jenoure, Roland Wiggins, and to Gwynelle Dismukes for helping me with the musical notations; and to James Baldwin for his encouragement.

Extra special thanks to William Strickland, who not only read the MS—but passed it on; and to Claudia Menza, who saw through it and then saw it through.

They do seem to be emerging . . . don't they, the little people of the play, all except that sly one, the chief figure, who draws farther and farther into the wood as we advance upon him? He so dislikes being tracked, as if there were something odd about him, that when he dies he means to get up and blow away the particle that will be his ashes.

* * *

He often wanders away alone with [his] weapon, and when he comes back you are never absolutely certain whether he has had an adventure or not. He may have forgotten it so completely that he says nothing about it; and then when you go out you find the body.

—J. M. Barrie,
*Peter Pan, or the Boy
Who Would Not Grow Up*

THE PETER PAN CHRONICLES

O N E

"There is a fixed number of energy streams," began Uncle Willie.

Parker had finally decided it was old Uncle Willie's grizzled visage in that corner. The image was a distillation of all the old men who had ever touched Parker's life: jovial, stern-faced, drunkard, professorial, sly-smiled and tisk-tisk—and all distant. Uncle Willie would do.

" . . . an unlimited number of possible *combinations* of energy streams, but a limited number of streams," Uncle Willie continued. "Some say twelve, like in the Zodiac, but four seems more likely. Even in the Zodiac you got your basic water, earth, wind, and fire. . . ."

Parker chuckled audibly as saliva trickled unnoticed down his chin.

The intern outside the door noticed. Patients like Raynard Parker caused her to seriously reevaluate her career choice. When she sneaked a look at this one's file she had seen a photo of him taken only a year before. Again she shivered in silent disbelief. His once sharp features were all but muted, as though his face had died. The eyes retained only an occasional claim on life and then only when he listened to or spoke to the voices and specters which seemingly cluttered his room.

"Poor dumb sonofabitch. He any better today?" The guard's question broke the silence with such severity that the intern thought that one of those voices had escaped Parker's room to confront her there in the hall.

"Ah, y—yes, he seems improved," she lied, her breath returning slowly. "Well, anyway, ah, we were able to remove his restraints this morning." The intern neglected to mention that Parker had also struck one of the doctors that very morning.

"So he's not still trying to jack himself off, huh?" The question was directed more to the intern's breasts than to the one-way glass on Parker's padded cell.

"No, the medication seems to be working." Then cautiously, "He's moved out of his favorite corner and more toward the center of the room. . . ." as she pushed by the guard.

"Four seems about right." Uncle Willie was rolling now. "Whether it's seasons or directions or the father, son, and the two holy ghosts. . . ."

"Which two?" Parker asked or thought he asked. His thoughts had so far outstripped the speed of his lips that the two resembled distant echos. He wasn't even sure if his vocal cords still worked, for his hearing was no longer like that of his keepers and the others. His faculties were probably only average for your run-of-the-litter psychotic, but for Parker everything had miraculously come together: sight, sound, taste, everything. Uncle Willie was definitely raspberry, a pungent raspberry.

Parker wondered how he tasted in Maggie's mouth and knew immediately that he was salty with his own secretions and hers. He could barely feel her now. Damned injections! But he could still taste her. And he could hear her soft sucking. He knew she had to be one of the two.

"Which two?" It was a woman's voice. It wasn't Maggie, Maggie was now running her tongue up and down his back. Or was that his own sweat he felt and tasted, trickling down his spine?

In another age, Parker would have been among the blessed. One touched by God, and thereby allowed to openly converse with his own gods—and demons. And a scribe, no doubt, would have been assigned to listen for those profundities which issued untainted from his lips.

America's black population still retains a high tolerance for crazy niggers, you know the trip: crazy niggers not knowing any better might actually *do* something.

No, that wasn't Maggie's voice. Even though she never said a word, Maggie did not sound like that. Parker knew that for sure. Must have come from the Forest directly in front of him.

He was always reluctant to glance over his right shoulder. Tommy Rollins was always sitting there grinning the way he was the first day Parker met him. But not quite. The mouth was different.

Could have been one of Rollins's women. But now why would they care? Parker sneaked a peek and there was grinning Tommy, like some skinny Buddha. The chill came suddenly, as always. Parker quickly refocused on Uncle Willie, who was still talking, as he had been for as long as Parker could recall.

"Throwing your voice again, Willie?" Parker eased into a chuckle.

Sometimes Uncle Willie seemed to have a slight German accent like some doctor Parker once talked to (Doc?) but never a woman's voice. No. It had to be coming from that damned Forest.

Now, it wasn't like there was only one forest in the room. Nope. Everything that ever existed on that spot seemed to still be there . . . trees, rocks, streams, people, monsters. Oh, yes, there is madness in myth. The descriptions of all those so-called mythical creatures were probably taken from the words of madmen and prophets, which is to say the same thing.

Trance-dance, madness, sleep, and death are all one, held together on the unicorn's horn.

* * *

Parker wondered why She, alone, wanted him to leave. Willie seemed to need an audience. Maggie would surely starve without him. And Rollins kept him around to rank and frighten. But She was always beckoning Parker toward the Forest, telling him he must move through, move on.

* * *

Too much clarity is the cause of cancer. His cells around the bubbling medication were as clear and conscious of themselves as they'd ever been. They were suddenly somebody!

Ego can grow irrespective of the common good. Parker sensed its beginning: the growing malignancy of the tumor with each new injection. Cancer grows where anonymity and ambiguity fade. . . .

(Four Times)

Hit—ain—eve—nin——Hal—mos—mor—nin——

(Breathy)
Hitainevenin   Halmosmornin
Hitainevenin   Halmosmornin
Hitainevenin   Halmosmornin
Hitainevenin   Halmosmornin

T W O

Parker caught a glimpse of Her once. A frightful sight. But somehow familiar. The eyes were familiar. The face was black serenity. The hair wasn't short or long but alive and Her body was fishlike: undulating shiny black scales. And She had this baby with Her, at least that's what Parker sensed. He couldn't really tell whether there was a baby or not or whether it was only him there at the scaly breast. He sensed that it—this baby—had arms and legs like a person and bowels and he was upside down eating and shitting at the same time. Or was it only the room that was upside down—again. Parker tried to concentrate on Uncle Willie's voice, but Rollins was clearer so Parker in desperation tuned that in:

"We always knew exactly who you were. We always knew. Some of us felt sorry for you. You were like some poor pitiful, incompetent superhero, some corny, costumed freak. A crypto faggot. That's what some folks thought about you. Just like those comic-book closet freaks. Secret identity has always been a code phrase for faggot. You gave eccentricity a bad name. The old folks had fun swapping lies with you. But the young ones got confused. They sometimes took you seriously. They were looking for the Truth, the correct posture. Your weirdness, your nuttiness in the name of blackness confused them. When we told them, some of them wanted to kill you. Others were skeptical and came and told you. That's when you decided you'd have them kill us. . . ."

KWEKU'S JOURNAL

5 April 1968

The world ended last night. . . .

KWEKU'S JOURNAL

5 August 1968

The world never ends. It just gets ugly.

T H R E E

WILLIE: *Now that first stream is a single, the second a double, the third a triple, and the fourth is a druple.*
PARKER: *Quadruple?*
WILLIE: *No! Druple!*

* * *

Conceived at the twilight's last gleaming, the final months of World War II and during the Jubilation II that followed, their hair set them apart. It was longer. Some of the people were fanatical about it, as converts often are. The natural/Afro/no-hot-comb-look wasn't a style. It was a statement.

The geriatric wards are already gearing up for them, figuring they will be hell-raisers. But what are they doing now, in between their righteous 1960s and their cane-wielding eighties to come?

"Maybe it was the tail of a comet that passed, bye-bye," mused Willie.

. . . When Jupiter aligns with Mars. . . . But the hair thing has become a generation marker with "long" men in their thirties and forties and "short" men in their teens and twenties. The stocking cap is back.

Willie asked: "You know how hard it is to make a stocking cap outta pantyhose?"

"Some are dead. . . ." said Rollins. He had been repeating it over and over again. But Parker had mistaken it for the sound of the generator that pushed fresh air into his room.

"And some are spies," laughed Willie.

"You know what makes a good spy good?" mocked Rollins.

"Yeah!" Parker shot back. "He can't play basketball."

"Patriotism!" shouted Willie. "The unshucked love of his god-damned-and-blessed-Europe's bastard of a country!"

"No, it was cynicism," whispered Rollins, knowingly.

". . . and ego," murmured the branches of the Corner Forest. Or was it Her voice?

What Parker did sense was the dissonant clang of tiny explosions in his left armpit. And then he knew. She had taught him something else: Ego is a cancer of the mind.

* * *

Basketball means not being afraid to dance with other men. But instead of graceful bodies gliding up and down the court, clustered about an elusive sphere, Parker saw only clunky shadows, shadows and kneecaps, and ankles pounded into hardwood mush, bone-splintered, joint-collapsed fingers and elbow-gouged, rage-blurred eyes.

His awkwardness had saved him and alienated him. Funny how one's stature increases with one's proficiency for putting a ball silently through hooped strings. . . . Funny also how Parker's alienation put him in touch and in tune with so many so-called leaders.

His awkwardness he'd overcome to the tune of a third-degree black belt. As for his alienation, hell, he didn't believe in that stuff.

No, it was from a small plant or perhaps it was three plants . . .

". . . more likely four," suggested Willie.

. . . that Parker learned the music of the spheres. He couldn't decide whether they were rooted in the floor of the Forest or in his own chest.

"Where are the free black men?"

"An illusion," intoned Doc.

"Look here. Here I am," smiled Willie, "free to do and say as I please. Free of the ties of position and possessions—"

"Slave catchers. You and slave catchers—a long history of upward mobility," Rollins hooted at Parker.

"Both of us free men," Parker volleyed.

"Free?"

"Yeah," Parker smiled as he moved toward the Forest.

"You don't want to go in there." It was Doc's voice.

"Why not?"

"There is treachery there, the very seat of illusion," cautioned Doc.

"You're just afraid to face me," taunted Rollins. "Running away again, right?"

Something snapped in Parker and he whirled about to face Rollins. He squinted at him and then slowly moved forward to get a better look.

Rollins's face was alive—with worms. Parker marveled at his own sudden loss of fear. He also marveled at the enhancement of his eyesight, for he saw not only worms but otherwise microscopic creatures at work on Rollins's face reducing it to its elements. "Decay is a party!" he thought he thought to himself. Or was that the wind too?

Parker moved closer, intrigued by the absence of stink. He did sense a moistness like humus though.

"Now what you gonna say, fool?" jeered Parker in a karate power stance.

"Incredible." Doc again. "It's as though he never heard a word I said."

"The male animal is incredible with his foot-stomping and branch-breaking displays."

Parker couldn't tell whether Doc was speaking to him, Willie, or his shrink notebook, as he was prone to do.

"Parker! You're the fool. This is no time for machismo. Can't you see you're confronting your own death?"

"You mean she's your mom too?" Parker heard himself ask as if he were trying to remember a conversation he was about to have.

"Nope, grandmother. And an anachronism. You'd call her 'old-timey.'" It seemed to be Willie's voice but sounded like some old familiar song sung without "voice."

"Hell, I'd call her Friday night if I had a phone and knew she was available." Parker heard his own fear break for the flip cover.

"But that's exactly the point, she's never 'available.' There is always some new infant at her breast. . . ." That had to be Rollins, or was it the clamor of the dewdrops at dawn jockeying for a choice spot on a blade of grace or grass?

Parker hadn't been this close to the edge since he'd lost it. He couldn't tell whether he was coming out of it or about to descend again. Maybe the thorazine was finally. . . . He felt literally high, as though he were so tall he could really see and hear those dewdrops bickering in the meadow beyond the hospital's grounds. He tried to control . . . control the drug by focusing on it the way She had taught him. As he concentrated he began to feel his feet back on the floor and discovered he was in Rollins's corner. But it was more an affirmation than a discovery. Somehow he had always been there, taunting Rollins and trying to ignore Doc's warnings. Yes, he knew he was slipping into something here. His own absence of fear was beginning to frighten him—but not quite. It was like his fear was on vacation, gone to Florida with the thorazine. He'd always counted on it, never was a slave to it, but trusted it as he had no other being, except maybe Rollins. And now it was gone.

"You hear that?" Parker confronted Rollins's lipless grin.

Rollins was finally silent as though waiting. "What you got to say about it, Uncle Willie?"

Again silence. For the first time in months he was without his voices.

Rollins's face began to fade. But before the image dispersed Parker let out a shattering cry as he delivered a death kick to the bridge of what used to be Rollins's nose.

The recoil was immediate. Parker felt himself soaring. He knew all at once that he had ruptured Rollins's methane envelope, sprained his own ankle, and struck a nerve in the wall.

The conversation was still going on. He heard his own voice the way it sounded on tape:

"You mean that both of you live here in the trees?" Parker sensed that he'd been blown to the treetops of the Corner Forest. He was addressing a presence hovering near him; it seemed to be Rollins. He wasn't sure.

"She is your mother and Willie's grandmother?"

"That's right." It had to be Rollins replying to both questions.

There was another presence also lingering there that seemed to be Willie, experienced but not heard. And hearing was different here, not really like a tape, not really voices . . . more like knowing.

There was no malice in this Rollins. Here was the Rollins Parker had known from the first. Old Tommy Smirk.

Euphoria was settling in. Without "moving" Parker had a full panoramic view of the complex and the surrounding West German countryside. And then it began to come back together:

"Kweku" Rollins. Parker was the only person who called him Tommy Smirk, first as a code name in reports to his G2 superiors and later to Rollins's face. Rollins seemed to take it in stride, even enjoyed the dub. It was as though he and Parker shared a secret about life's absurdities.

Parker had always expected Rollins to break out in a belly laugh any minute now. He seemed ever on the verge but he never did, never even showed his teeth—except for that once. Parker checked him out when he spoke or ate just to make sure he had teeth. It was a running joke between them.

Rollins's house was always jumping, what with the two women and five kids. There was a lot of speculation about that too. Some thought the women were prostitutes and that Rollins was a thinking man's procurer. One of the women seemed ten years Rollins's senior. The other looked to be a few years his junior, but such things are often difficult to tell with black folk. Three of the kids couldn't have been Rollins's, didn't look anything like him, and had last names other than his and the two women's.

To outsiders, the house was alive with children of all ages and shades, food cooking, and famous folk coming and going. Those famous folks were mainly black political figures and spokespersons who came to address the local college where Rollins taught. Some of them stopped there going and coming on their way to New York and points north and south.

These "names" were what first attracted Parker to that house and to Rollins. However, what began as surveillance soon became what Parker thought was a friendship. When, in heated late-night discussions, Rollins's guests accused Parker of spreading confusion, Rollins stepped in to protect his eccentric friend, even though he knew that Parker needed no such protection. In fact, one of Parker's ploys was to provoke certain of the more militant names into physical confrontation so he could humiliate them by busting a couple of their ribs in the alley behind Rollins's house. The more he did it the more transparent it became, until finally Rollins had only to frown at him and Parker would immediately take a more conciliatory tack.

Parker's respect for Rollins grew with each visit to that house, especially as he began to decipher how it was organized. Under his guise as perennial grad student, Parker bummed many a meal at Rollins's table—or Rema's table, to be technical. Rema Douglas, AKA Rema DuBois, the older of the two women, lived on the first floor of the house (three bedrooms, kitchen, bath, full dining room) with her two teenaged sons and a three-year-old daughter. It was at her table that everyone gathered on Sundays and feast days. Official sources, that is, Parker's sources, confirmed that she had indeed once briefly been a prostitute—and a dancer and a pianist and a cosmetologist, and a waitress and. . . . She later told Parker that she had merely been dancing in the wrong club at the wrongest time. Now she did cornrowing and taught dance at the book-fabric-jewelry store and day-care center in the converted storefront Rollins rented near the house. The younger woman, Janet Fields, lived in the upstairs apartment (three bedrooms, one of which was occupied by Rema's oldest son, kitchen, bath) with her ten-year-old daughter and two-year-old baby girl. She had a B.A. in sociology, did sub work in the public schools, part-time secretarying and, when she could, taught four-year-olds in the storefront how to read. Parker had flirted with her from the first day, her and Rema.

Rema had told him he was full of it, but Janet had flirted right back and right in front of Rollins, who, of course, smirked.

Fact was Rollins never did have much to say—except on the lecture circuit, where he probably said too much and in his BS classes. Parker had a running list of what these initials stood for: Blame (&) Shame, Blast (&) Stab, Burn (&) Sack, Blimpe Sub (full of gas), Blow-Shot (likewise), Bilious Snot, and Bravo Sambo, to name a few. Of course, given a choice, Parker went with the most obvious association, while Rollins preferred Buckra Shuck to any of these, as might have been obvious from his course titles: "BS 223: The Political Economy of the American Recording Industry" and "BS 400 (Special Topics): If Marx and Mao had Made the Middle Passage." Like Parker, Rollins was a watcher, a listener. When he did speak, it was always with great authority and assurance.

The high and would-be mighties came by to use Rollins as a sounding board for some outrageous schemes. And Rollins never minced words with them no matter who it was. If it was crap, he told them just that. Or was that Rema's voice? It seemed as though she or Janet were always there, there in the basement apartment where Rollins lived, where the Young Turks, would-be mighties, and names gathered. Even harsh objections raised by the men's talk would-be-war advocates were met with a quiet explanation from old Tommy Smirk about who lived in the house and who was *only* visiting and with the hospitality of whom. Over time the women did become less vocal, but by then they and Rollins had developed a system of winks, raised eyebrows, frowns, and the like which Rollins also used on Parker.

But nobody dared shut up Uncle Willie. Hell, Willie was the representative of *the community*. Willie was a part-time wino (when his Social Security check was on time) who had a room someplace in the city but spent many a night on a cot in the back of Rollins's basement. He might have even been a relative of one of the occupants. (Rema and her brood called him Poppa Willie.) Anyway, Willie definitely had a few things to say about the First War and the last days in time, about woolly-headed young folk having no respect, about the Coptic, the price of wine, and the President's bowel movements.

* * *

WILLIE: *Sound is the key. In the proper pitch. You know, like pitchin' horseshoes, the arch has to be just so. Then the yoni hugs tight on the spike so's you get that ringer's ring, clear and high. Sound is the doorway between worlds known and unknown. Tone and inflection can turn nigger-shit into nigger-love. Same letters. Different turns on the up-going and the down-coming, that's all.*
   Sound.
   That's why them priests and priestesses of old was always *musicians. Man, they knew the chords! Ones to take you 'way from here and ones to bring you back. They was also the dance masters 'cause they had* all *the steps. . . .*

* * *

About those women. Sometimes they were like sisters, sometimes like lovers. Sometimes rivals, and sometimes Rema played big mama to Janet's shy-daughter act.

Were they lovers? Parker's superiors seemed to take a perverse interest in that—an interest which Parker sustained.

Rema consistently took things right to the edge. Parker knew that for sure. And Janet certainly was pliant enough.

The two of them together in a threesome with Rollins would have been hot! Where would all the hands go? The mouths?

Parker had to ask, and more than once. And each time, Rema rocked and laughed from the deep, holding her sides—the only way you *can* laugh at a fool who'll never know.

Then she'd just give him a green-eyed glare until he was forced to look away.

KWEKU'S JOURNAL

5 December 1968

Today I made a career choice: teacher. This in spite of last night's dream.

Somebody named Ol' Cap'n was speaking to me from far off. Then he was smiling and patting me on the back: "Boy, you do that. You teach. Here, you want books? How about office space? Got enough spending money, boy?"

F O U R

They say that men can know a kind of friendship women cannot imagine. Unfortunately, men can't imagine it either. And without imagination, there is no expression.

Rollins, Parker, and James gathered thus encumbered late one night in Rema's kitchen. James sat tall with these men, who had rebuffed Rema's efforts to hustle him off at half past bedtime. Parker was grateful for the room's relaxed air. For an instant, he almost felt safe. And Rollins was trying to think of some way to thank Ray for suggesting the title of his latest paper, "Black Studies and Other Male Fantasies," without endorsing Parker's cynicism. Because he was tired, Rollins didn't feel up to the argument that his positive approach to fantasies would certainly evoke from Parker. Instead, he winked at Ray and offered a smirky grin.

Parker immediately stiffened and, though he managed a careful smile, his eyes, without their perennial dark glasses, betrayed uncertainty.

Rollins placed a firm and reassuring hand on Parker's shoulder as he rose to secure a couple more beers from the fridge. Ray relaxed—a little. Perhaps the wink was in response to James's adulation of the latest John Shaft movie. James was still rattling on about it, even though he knew Rollins disapproved of the genre. "I'd do street theater for coins tossed in a hat before I'd let Ho'Wood ream me like that," Rollins had snorted.

"Oh, really?" Parker finally had his turn at bat. "You'd prefer talcum to vaseline?"

James loved it. This thing between Kweku and Ray, it was like a game that neither could lose—but that wasn't the point/goal, anyway. "It" wasn't about score. Rollins was the smartest, kindest, most serious man James had ever known. Even his mother's nocturnal trips to Rollins's bed no longer bothered James. Kweku was the first one who made it seem right. And Parker! Parker sometimes seemed even smarter than Rollins. He sure knew more practical stuff. Like how to kill somebody with your hands and feet. James didn't care what Poppa Willie or anybody said. Parker was definitely badder than Shaft.

* * *

The smell of linoleum, that was Rema's kitchen for the longest time. Rollins had suggested tile but no, Rema insisted that a kitchen needed linoleum. Affordable.

Ray argued that a pot of chittlins with a pot of cabbage on the side were the only antidotes for that fresh linoleum smell. Politically incorrect, but effective. So what if the combined odors killed someone? As far as he knew, even the U.S. had never banned chem-warfare.

F I V E

Parker remembered the time he'd actually convinced a black professor of his inferiority compared to his white colleagues, how his scholarship was shoddy, his publishers questionable, and how his "professional black-caucus organizations" were just drinking clubs. He had expected at least an attempt at a rebuttal but none showed. The prof was naked, found out. He had been half-stepping all his life. Parker tried to suggest alternative standards of excellence but realized that half-stepping is a habit worse than any. Even as a rootworker the prof would probably be slipshod.

But maybe not, with other assumptions or standards clearer, as clear as death. "Hey, you can't be no halfway shaman, no almost initiate—you is or you ain't, and if you ain't you're dead tryin'." Or if you're like the prof you'd see that it is just as honorable and a hell of a lot safer sweeping the temple stairs. Commitment. Rollins's "rules" for spies came back to Parker. "You're either in or out. Nothing halfway. If you're gonna do the white boy thing do it to the max. Don't just wear the trappings, mouth the lines, play the part. No. Do it! Be it!"

Halfway and what have you got?

". . . just another nigger professional, or is that backwards?" the prof had scrawled just before he ventilated his skull.

His was the first voice Parker had heard when he had his "breakdown." The prof wailed for Parker to take his own life. And Parker almost had.

S I X

ROLLINS: *We only get to see Her breast and stomach, sometimes the underside of Her chin. Every man knows that to see Her face-to-face you have to take your body along. You can meet Her, make Her only in the flesh.*
PARKER: *What about Maggie?*
ROLLINS: *What does she look like?*
PARKER: *I, ah, I don't recall. No. I don't know. Never knew to recall.*
ROLLINS: *That's because you've never seen Her.*
PARKER: *And where do I meet Her?*
ROLLINS (indicating the Forest floor): *Down there.*

S E V E N

Shortly after the American Embassy was seized, most of the women and blacks were released. They say that when Ray Parker's young captors offered him this option of oppressed status and immediate release, part of his outraged and outrageous response/performance was fueled by his genuine hatred for the whole concept of oppression. Sho-nuff slaves had never seen themselves as oppressed in the self-indulgent, pity-me-please way that rights-seeking, so-called revolutionaries of the 1960s had. Parker had disrupted many a "political" meeting with several variations on that indignation: "Slaves were more in tune with the old African sensibility about rights than you clowns! They knew that rights aren't something that another can give or take." Why he lapsed into that particular variation at *that* time was certainly a mystery to his captors, who hardly understood his words but clearly saw madness in his exaggerated gestures and tone, while his colleagues thought he'd certainly been drinking.

Had Parker been a mere embassy file clerk he could have safely professed his undying devotion to God and country and remained in captivity. But as G2, his job was to shuffle his oppressed buns on out of there—with those sensitive documents still on him if possible.

Parker's other options were to collaborate—for real (imagine the old Ninth Cavalry fighting on Geronimo's side, good God!)—or conversely to double-agent the hell out of his captors. He did neither. He went crazy, when the crazy-nigger routine wasn't even on the program.

At some point in his ravings, Parker heard Her voice for the first time, as She pulled him to Her. He'd mocked the moon once too often. She reminded him that the tease was Her province, not his.

Parker's lapse, er, indiscretion, er, breakdown was an embarrassment for all concerned. The documents on him implicated him as at least a collaborator in the Intelligence Community. That implication put a kink in his captors' propaganda line—well, he *was* black—and ripped the blanket spy-denial off Parker's employers.

Still raving, Parker was stripped and confined. He injured himself several times and his screams were unnerving. His captors, claiming a lack of proper facilities, were understandably pleased with the opportunity to release Parker for medical reasons. They say he was heavily sedated during a clandestine flight to a military hospital in West Germany. Parker's voices had obviously taken an earlier flight. They were there to greet him.

It took awhile for them to jell into four or five he could consistently recognize. At the start they were a jangle of the recent, local, and long dead and a jumble of disembodied beings too weak to incarnate on their own. These latter attached themselves leechlike on all the newly mad. Parker fought them off. Even in his ravings he reflexed on the mental tricks he'd mastered during his training: he ignored them; he wolfed at them; he pitted them one against the other. The dead, however, remained clustered about him. Many took no notice of him and he extended them the same favor. Others chided him Willie-style: "Boy, just 'cause you been boogered don't mean you got to booger others."

Aborted babies floated by, cussin' like longshoremen. A million murdered Jews marched back and forth through the room. And though they shouted, "Never again!" they, nonetheless, kept on marching, just marching. Vengence seekers, suicides, hanged criminals, gutted soldiers, gray heads wandered about, passing through one another and Parker.

Parker held his own against them all, all except the blacks betrayed by blacks. "Boy, what's wrong wit' you? Git up and face us. Nigga, get up!"

As specters they couldn't harm him. Part of him knew that. Knew it. But Rollins's voice rising above the throng chilled Parker to the core.

He retreated to Maggie's corner. . . .

E I G H T

WILLIE: *Who is this Maggie he always moans about in his sleep? Must be someone who comes in the night and leaves 'fore day. She don't even ruffle the sheets. Pure pleasure, no grief. Hey, somebody come and wake this nigger 'fore he hurt his self!*

PARKER: *Oommm, you are Maggie. Your touch is magic. . . .*

WILLIE: *Hey! Somebody wake him 'fore I have to hurt him!*

DOC: *Well, names* do *get slurred during dreams. But obviously* Maggie *is the ultimate abstraction: woman reduced to touch, woman reduced to soft hands and willing mouth. It's certainly not magic you can sustain in daylight.*

PARKER
&
WILLIE: *Oh?*

(Four Times)

It ain't eve- nin'——Al—mos' mor-nin'——

It ain't evenin' Almos' mornin'
It ain't evenin' Almos' mornin'
It ain't evenin' Almos' mornin'
It ain't evenin' Almos' mornin'

KWEKU'S JOURNAL

5 January 1970

The Revolution never came. Black folks got gunned and gassed for days. But the Revolution never came. The fires of rebellion wrought only the cooling effects of poverty pimping and votes for black mayors. Every dangerously charismatic figure has been silenced: killed, co-opted, imprisoned, or exiled.

The Revolution never came. And an entire generation now sit with their guns loaded, their 'myte stored, waiting . . . afraid. It is a fear which drives us to the brink of madness.

Did we think that It would come like some wet dream in the night?

N I N E

WILLIE: *You got to admit the man had grace.*

PARKER: *Yeah, and Rema and Janet and who knows how many others? Look, as far as women are concerned, a man's got to choose. It's a wonder those biddies didn't put out a contract on the bastard themselves. The man who won't choose is a doomed man.*

WILLIE: *You know them times when you just can't eat enough, drink enough, smoke enough? Did I say drink enough?*

PARKER: *Yeah.*

WILLIE: *It ain't body hunger. No, it's deeper'n that.*

DOC: *Women, even the professional ones, deep down, think that a man will eventually fill that hole—the one left when they subtract their children, their work, and other women. I think men always knew better. But maybe that's only the "man's reality" again.*

WILLIE: *Well, men ain't dragged about on that wheel of the moon. And it's hard to feel completely alone when you're on the same trip with flowers, frogs, and furry bats and shit—not to mention them rhythm ripples we call tides.*

DOC: *Yes, well, men have cycles too. . . .*

WILLIE: *Oh, yeah, them empties come about once a month when you begin to miss your, your . . . whatchacallit?*

DOC: *Ovaries?*

WILLIE: *Right, every normal creature used to have 'em.*

PARKER: *And balls too?*

WILLIE: *Sure. Yeah, them too.*

PARKER: *And you the ball-snatcher?*

WILLIE: *And you the ovary-crusher?*

PARKER: *Not me. It wasn't me. Honest, it wasn't me!*

T E N

On the morning that the blacks (in this instance men) and women (as always "white") were to be released from the embassy, Clemmons, one of the black Marines, had asked for and was given permission to see Parker. Lance Corporal Clemmons wasn't certain why he wanted to see this man whose name he didn't know. The "*Bad* Man," he and the others respectfully called Parker.

"Hey, the 'Bad Man' kicks ass!"

"Yeah, he don't cut *no* slack. You hear him tell 'em?"

"Yeah, but what, ah, what exac'ly did he say?"

All Clemmons knew for sure was that he was leaving and Parker was staying. And somehow leaving didn't . . . well, he couldn't put his finger on it.

Parker huddled naked in a corner of his empty room. He glared at the slight figure before him but may not have actually seen or heard Clemmons at all. Parker did speak to him though, or to someone:

"No, no. Go. You go on now. It's all right. Look, you ignorant bastard, you'll live to die another day. Don't worry 'bout it!"

Parker could no longer filter thoughts from speech so every thought, his or maybe Clemmons's, immediately became sound.

"Hey, look, initially you might get some shit assignments. But those will pass. Sure, at first it'll look suspect on your record. But in a few years it'll just read 'Captured and Released' . . . ambiguous. Leave the interpretation for the bone pickers—what they call themselves? Oh, yeah—his and her storians.

"I know you're a damn good Marine, a *damn* good Marine! I know that. You know that. But that don't make no difference—*never* made any difference. Hey, who the hell remembers the Chicago Eight Ball, bound, gagged, and gone?"

"The Chicago what?"

"Well, the Seven ain't that hip no mo' eitha, and likewise bein' a captive ain't gonna be big shit neither pretty soon, you watch. No, you'll live to die another day. Count on it.

"Oh, yeah, I can dig it, it makes you feel 'funny' that you've made friends with some of these 'revolutionaries,' our delightful hosts. And them hostesses? Man, some of 'em are downright *fine!* Oh, yeah! But that's alright, 'cause you always make friends, sometimes you make babies, but you always make friends—gooks in the southeast, red-hide niggers in the southwest—go 'head, learn the 'Fu, wear the moccasins, but keep steppin', you hear me?"

"Yes, Sir!"

"No, that's, that's alright. 'Cause you know where you're headin'. Dontcha?"

"Yes, Sir!"

"I can't hear you!"

"YES, SIR!"

"You know you're on the right side, the *winnin'* side. And winnin's what it's all about. Am I right?"

"Yes, Sir!"

"Say what?"

KWEKU'S JOURNAL

5 July 1971

Tracks: As Recounted by Ray

Last night I had a dream.

Me and the boys was out cruisin' on one of the main ghetto drags in D.C., Florida Avenue. You know Florida Avenue, up there where the streetcars used to run? Most of the tracks are still there. Ain't no streetcars run since 1960, but all over the city you still find tracks.

Anyway, we was cruisin' in the lefthand lane—on the tracks. We had started out in that old Chevy I used to own, but by the time we'd hit the Big Avenue the car had been somehow transformed.

I suddenly discovered I was driving something more sleek and close to the ground. There was no power under my feet. All the propulsion seemed to come from the rear—from the periodic pushing of my "crew." We were seated in what amounted to a toboggan. But there was no snow, not in July. Everything else seemed normal, though. The radio was blastin'. And the brothers in the back was yellin' at them fine sisters paradin' the sidewalks. Sayin' things like: "Hey, baby, can I go with you?" "You don't want to *do* nothin', do you?" "Well, you ain't got to speak, Bitch!"

Before too long, or even at the same time—only folks who are alive or awake, make such distinctions—I was compelled to slow down. The "short" did have brakes. There had been an accident up ahead in the lefthand lane.

Two or three dog-pound trucks, turned every which-a-way, had spewn their contents all over the street. For three blocks the streets were covered with bits and pieces of dog flesh. The animals had been torn to shreds. Policemen waded shin-deep in entrails and blood, directing traffic. Some old high-ballin' freight train had got loose on the streetcar tracks and just plowed right through them trucks.

Apparently we weren't moving fast enough 'cause one of the cops came over, grabbed the steering wheel, and began to pull us around the wreckage. I sat back with my foot on the brake and watched this other plainclothes cop across the way, his cheap suit splattered with blood, direct a crane into position.

And then we saw the bear. Right there in the middle of Florida Avenue, there in the midst of all those dead dogs, in fact with dogs crushed beneath it, clinging to it, impaled on its fangs and claws, was a full-grown grizzly bear—also quite dead. Nearby there were two smaller bears which had likewise apparently died in combat.

I looked away from the carnage. Glancing down at my own splattered shirt front, I rejoiced that dreams have no scent. . . .

"Imagine," began Brother Poet, sitting directly behind me. "Imagine how it must have been for those poor dogs caught in the middle of a cataclysm and then set upon by bears. But they sure gave them hell!"

Another story was being told at the next corner, however. Seated atop a mailbox was the man-first-on-the-scene.

"The she-bear and her cubs they was crossin' the street—with the light, mind you—when the dogs, half-crazy with starvation and fear climbed outa the wreckage. Straight away they made for the cubs. Like wolves, the dogs was on them. That's when that old she-bear stood up, arms out like this. And with tears in her eyes she screamed: 'Murderers! You're killing my children!' She took off most of them dogs all by herself, too, before the cops came and shot her. . . ."

The brothers behind me began to kick. The wind rushed cold in my face and I awoke.

ELEVEN

DOC: *It may be impossible to do other than what we do, be other than what we are. Impossible.*
WILLIE: *Impossible?*
PARKER: *Few energy streams, very few. Willie's right!*
WILLIE: *Impossible?*
DOC: *This time this place this "world" is caught up in the force of the eternal boy. Can't break out.*
WILLIE: *Say what?*
DOC: *There may be* only *boys. All that Madonna-with-male-child statuary may be the key.*
PARKER: *Rebellious boys . . .*
WILLIE: *Sheeit!*
PARKER: *What?*
WILLIE: *Never did pay to be too white-boy-smart* and *black. Could go crazy easy. Wisdom always has a context: wise in the way of this or that. . . .*
DOC: *Even your Malcolm and your Martin operated out of the* puer aeternus *mode, like two mythical brothers, one bent toward the earth, the other toward the sky. It doesn't even matter which was which. Their respective striving, their struggling toward the heights and the depths was in that mode.*
PARKER: *Hmmmmm. . . .*
WILLIE: *"Mode"/"context," you see what I mean? Rebellious what?! Funny thing about ridin' night trains with the lights on: in order to see anything out there in the dark you gotta look through the reflection of your own face. A lot of folks find that impossible.*

TWELVE

Somewhere Parker knew that *he'd* never denied Rollins a chance for his own in-the-flesh meeting with Her. Rollins, all by himself, had had that chance way back in sixty-nine—some two years before Ray descended on him. Rollins had chosen to transpersonalize that opportunity and so had lost it. What Kweku gained was two women.

Parker heard Rollins talk about it once, or at least Ray thought he had. Now the voice sounded very much like his own:

"It doesn't matter what you do in this country. When you do it well and, heaven forbid, when you begin to like it, you're done for. You're in their pocket with the other 'goods': chewing gum, cigarettes, niggers. Even if you do nothing, you're in their pocket.

"The trouble with us is that we didn't all die, not on the boat nor in the fields nor in the streets. But once we knew we weren't dead, we had only one option that would have ripped a hole in the pocket. That was to kill those mother-rapers. Do *that* well! The other option was to kill that part of ourselves that couldn't live with the contradictions. A lot of us turned the blade inward, embroidered the goddamned pocket, and created a whole culture out of cigarette butts and shoe-stuck gum.

"But there's always a third option. Willie'd probably argue for a fourth. But we know there's at least a third. That was to embrace the contradictions, to risk splitting ourselves in two just to hold them all to our bosom. Those of us who can't do that on our own try to live with those who can, who do it all the time—who *are IT!*"

* * *

WILLIE: *Hey, you! Yeah, I'm talkin' to you! Boy, let me tell you somethin'. You been a outside/inside agitator for as long as I been knowin' you, and I been knowin' you since you was a baby, back when you used to kill people just to bring 'em back to life.*

Showoff! Now *look at you—hangin' out with whores, drinkin' wine with the rabble (present company excluded), rumblin' in the temple (of all places), singin', dancin', and raisin' hell among country and city folk alike. You better watch yourself, boy, or you gonna wake up one of these mornin's with your ass nailed to a damn tree!*

THIRTEEN

Between trips to the Coast, where he served as "full-time" security chief for a Bay Area liberation group, Parker spent almost three years hanging out at Rollins's house. He taught Rema and her boys how to fight and the oldest boy, James, how to shoot.

Parker even babysat the three girls on those rare occasions when everyone else was out.

He felt like a part of the family. Hell, he knew almost everything about them. He knew that Rosemary and Jamila (Janet's oldest and Rema's youngest) couldn't stomach G-rated movies but were definitely into the heavy R's, especially the horror flicks. And that it didn't matter at all to baby Amina, who just slept through it all. He knew that Rema's younger son, Jerome, had been to the juvenile detention center on drug and petty-larceny charges. He knew that James was the baddest ass-kicking sixteen-year-old he'd ever encountered. The kid picked up on everything Parker had to offer—hand-to-hand, stick fighting, you name it. And that James was a dead shot at twenty feet, which was about the optimum range for Janet's old rickety .22 pistol. Parker knew that when Janet accompanied Rollins on speaking engagements, which certainly seemed more frequent since the article had been published, she often took the .22 along.

So Parker, full of information and not a little miffed at Rollins, figured his was the only gun in the house that snowy Saturday morning in February seventy-four. He lay there naked in Rema's bed listening to her in the kitchen down the hall scolding the little girls, who were then about four and five, about their sloppy table manners and instructing Rosemary on the proper way to stir grits. Parker thumbed through Rollins's article again. He could almost recite it from memory by then, but he still hadn't figured out the why's of it.

The Means of Production   December 1973

DEADLY CON MEN:
BLACK AGENTS PROVOCATEURS OF THE 1960S

Introduction

Recently the news media have begun to reveal the extent to which the components of the Intelligence Community (FBI, CIA, G2 units of the various armed services, and undercover units of local police departments) were involved in the surveillance and manipulation of the Rights, Nationalism, and Anti-War Movements of the 1960s. Little in-depth analysis has been done, however, of the peculiar role which black agents played in these activities.

What follow are the first steps toward such an analysis. This effort is, of course, hampered from the very beginning by its own subjectivity. Although there are a few references to published accounts, most of what follows is based on the lingering suspicions, observations, and intuitions of this writer.

For those of us who were even peripherally involved in efforts to alter the structure and priorities of American Society, the real legacy of the all-pervasive intelligence activities of the 1960s is a nagging suspicion that perhaps some of our best friends and closest associates were spies.

Why had Rollins done it? Sure, black nationalist publications had put the government's business in the streets as far back as '71, but the national media wouldn't pick up on it until the smoke cleared in about another decade. Now here was Rollins right in the middle of it, strapping this bull's-eye to his back. Why? Was it Rema? "You found out about me and Rema? Hey, man, it wasn't nothin'. Look, some reefer and maybe three minutes at the outside. And we only did it about three or four times in two years! You're a homebody, remember?" For an instant, Parker was back in the trees. And there was silence.

"Why then?" he shouted.

Rema poked her head in the door with a puzzled expression. "You call?"

Parker waved her away, then called after her: "Where's my piece?"

"Where it belongs." As usual he had left his gun on the nightstand and as usual she had removed it to the top shelf of the hall closet, "out of the reach of the kids."

"Hurry now, your breakfast is ready!" over her shoulder as she flip-flopped back to the kitchen.

"In a minute. . . ." Parker turned the page.

Profile and Motivation of the Black Spy

Generally, black agents appeared to be highly motivated, intelligent individuals with a sharp eye for detail. If they were members of service units, they probably volunteered for their undercover assignments. Those involved with student movements were often older and more mature in appearance than their contemporaries and they used this to enhance their position as authority figures and leaders with long experience in movement activities.

Agents, even when they acknowledged the racial inequities within the ranks of their own service organizations, seem to have been sincerely convinced that the United States of America was the best place on the planet for blacks to be. Blacks who disagreed and who endeavored to verbally or physically express their dissatisfaction with the quality of their existence were viewed as dangerously sick.

Those agents recruited from the ranks of black academia (administrators, faculty, students) seemed to share this view. They believed in the principle of racial equality, but saw many of the pursuits of student activists, especially their call for the development of a separate Black Nation, as treasonous.

Patriotism seems therefore to have been a binding force and source of inspiration for many black agents. There were others, however, who were attracted by the sense of personal power which being a spy afforded. Among this latter group were active criminals who allowed themselves to be pressed into service to avoid criminal prosecution. They were often given immunity from further prosecution while they worked as agents, and virtually had licenses to kill.

This power of life and death, along with the ability to manufacture reality, seems to have been an important part of the metaphysical attractiveness of being a black spy.

One of Parker's superior officers was once heard to remark: "These nigger agents are in a difficult position, sure, but they know on which side their bread is buttered. They're no fools. Yeah, they're still niggers, but some of the brightest ones I've ever met."

* * *

When he finally broke it off with Doris on the Coast (it must have been a couple of months before Rollins's "exposé"), Parker started attending conferences there designed specifically to address the "Problem" between black men and black women. The Problem, this thing, appeared actually to be a latticework of loaded questions: Why is he so triflin' and irresponsible? Why is she so impenetrable and sharp of tongue? And why, oh why can't they get together, be together, stay together? Huh?

It was at one of these conferences that he met Drs. Jacob and Rachael Sieber, a pair of clinical psychologists, who were appearing on two of the panels. Rachael's panel was on sexual technique, with films and everything. But Parker found Jake Sieber's presentation more stimulating.

Doc! He suddenly remembered who Doc was. "Where's Doc?" Parker asked the wind. No reply. He sensed that Doc had no connection with the trees. . . .

Yeah, Doc Sieber. Sieber caught a lot of flack at that conference, him and his fairy tales. Parker couldn't quite recall what his talk was about—something to do with Peter Pan being a metaphor for modern man and *that* Problem not being a black or white issue. "Wendy always grows up, but Pan is just Pan, a boy-smile on a wheel, 'round and back."

Parker liked the little man and his feistiness. He rose to Sieber's defense with an eloquent argument drawn from his own experience, which he could now no longer remember. Nothing like a big argument to disrupt a meeting—and Parker did have to keep in practice.

After the conference, Parker started seeing Sieber to talk about the Doris break and a few other personal things. He still went to the conferences though, to pick up on the ladies. He finally figured out that that was what those gatherings were really about.

Parker felt comfortable with Sieber and probably told him too much.

Sieber asked him point-blank why he'd become a spy and not simply a social critic. Parker vehemently responded that social critics were merely fat-assed article factories.

"The only place for what you'd call a 'man of action' in *this* society—the only place for *me* to have learned what I know is in the service—special forces at that!"

"Have you done a tour in Vietnam?"

"All my assignments have been Stateside, except for short hops to France and Germany."

"Well, why haven't you applied your skills to aid the armed struggle of your people?"

Parker immediately rose and began checking Sieber's office for bugs. "Is that a rhetorical question?"

"Certainly not."

"Who are you to ask me that? What armed struggle? A couple of heroes in Cleveland gunned down by black FBI agents? Those chinaman-quoting cowboys in Oakland and Chicago, who dressed up to be executed? What struggle? Hell, the deck was stacked from jump street to D.C. Costumes, gestures, peashooters, bold talk against computers and enough firepower to fuel World War III? What struggle? What warriors?

"The only warrior tradition in America since the indigenous folk bowed their heads has been in the armed forces. And even the Devil deserves some loyalty if he gives you the skills to be what you're destined to be. Besides—"

"Destined?" Sieber's eyebrows rose.
"Besides. . . ."

* * *

No, Rollins was wrong. There was just no other place for Parker to be to thrive. "Metaphysics? What is this shit?" Parker turned the page.

The Metaphysics and Sociology of Spying

"Tell a big enough lie, loud and long enough, and it becomes as good as true." Or so the paraphrased saying goes. Certainly since World War I, nations have employed all forms of propaganda, i.e., exaggerated truths, half-truths, bold-faced lies, in their inter- and intranational struggles. Every agent in the 1960s probably learned early in his career just how pliant reality could be.

National, state, and local governments each had their own vision of how a black revolutionary should look and sound. Agents attempted to mirror that image. Some real, or at least potentially real, black revolutionaries liked the image enough to imitate it. As new leaders emerged, agents incorporated the style of these into the general revolutionary repertoire and the mirroring continued.

Such mirroring went on until the images of the real and the imitation revolutionary became so entwined as to be indistinguishable.

From the recent revelations of the almost complete manipulation of the German Intelligence Network during World War II by British/American Intelligence, to Malcolm X's revelations of how the 1963 March on Washington was transformed by the Kennedy Administration from a grass-roots rebellion to a festive media event, the pattern of government thinking is the same: It is not always as important to stop something as it is to control it.

In controlling and manipulating the various segments of the Black Liberation Movement of the 1960s, black agents were at a decided advantage. While blacks generally were struggling for an identity and a sense of direction, black agents had the security of self-created identities and direction from higher-ups. Moreover, the agents had the personal freedom to act which comes from the loss of one's personal history. Agents were whoever they wanted to be whenever they wanted to be, while at the same time they maintained a secret sense of self.

Power and authority naturally accrues to even partially self-realized persons. In this regard, agents were as wolves among sheep. To blacks seeking political gurus and revolutionary saviors, many agents appeared to be the embodiment of answered prayers.

Ironically, agents were probably among the few blacks in America competent enough to be "real" revolutionaries. Specifically, the agents knew where the guns were, how to get them, and how to use them. Because of their contingency planning, they knew how and if revolutionary activities might be accomplished. They knew where to attack, with what strength, and where to hide. They were probably often impatient with the lack of skill and insight and the hollow rhetoric of black leaders with whom they worked.

"How you figure he know all that?" Two young brothers confronted Parker with a copy of *Production* two days after the Rollins issue came out.

"Hey, man, like I don't know. Maybe Kweku be spyin' on the spies." Parker gave them grinning nonchalance.

"Or maybe he beez one hissef," they interrupted.

"Well, that's just too thick for me to *even* deal with. Could be . . . but like, hey, what can I say? Say, look, brothers, I got to split. Check you at the meetin' tonight?"

"Right, Ahmed. Later on." The young men turned to one another with hands on their chins like the elders they might never become.

Parker gave them his back and his patented "polio glide" down the block. Turning the corner and the page, he still couldn't figure what Rollins was trying to accomplish.

The Language of the Black Spy: Wolf Tickets and the Emperor's New Clothes

Black agents often spoke in cliché-riddled rhetorical gobbledygook—just like a lot of other people during that period. But the agents' gobbledygook was deliberately designed to obscure, divide, and confuse. They seemed to promote the most outlandish and ridiculous ideas and behavior patterns in the name of blackness. And, of course, those of us who were afraid of being blacker-than-thou'ed promptly fell in line.

Another pattern that was observed even among white agents, especially those involved in the antiwar movement, was a periodic tendency to make deliberately self-revealing statements. It was almost as though the deception sometimes became too burdensome.

For example, in 1971, a friend of mine, whom I later came to suspect as a spy, turned to me and said, "In order for a black man to be successful in America, he has to betray his people." Out of the clear blue, he said that and then looked away.

When Parker admitted to his superiors that he had, indeed, made that remark about success, they strongly suggested he confine his activities to the Coast for awhile. Parker dutifully extended his grad-school-leave extension, quit his library job, and settled into the group-grope gatherings and Sieber sessions. He once asked Jake if he and Rachael discussed the Parker case before or after they had intercourse at night. Sieber said, "Before," never blinking.

But all the while the Rollins article gnawed at Parker. Sure, Parker had black folks looking to Venus and Mars and Middle Earth for their ancestors. But he and Rollins had laughed about that stuff, laughed and drunk wine with Willie. Or had it only been Willie who was laughing? Rollins *had* talked about how blacks were changing, becoming more literal-minded like their teachers, and how sad that was. But Parker was certain that Rollins had at least smiled after that, smiled the way he always did. Yeah, he even spoke of a fable he'd written.

* * *

WILLIE: *That's right, you right. Niggers and cockroaches came down here together in the tail of the* comet Venus. *And by the time Venus had got Herself together, we had already turned this*

mother out! Charmed the moon, chained the sun, and kicked hell outta the dinosours!
PARKER: *Those cockroaches are pretty tough, huh?*

* * *

"What was Tommy Smirk trying to say to me? Was it 'Come on home, brother, it's alright, we got your number, come on, it's cold out there'? Was it that? But this is my job, man, my life. I figured you understood that." For a moment he was back in the trees. "You understood so much. Didn't you know that for months I fed the white boys false information just so I could continue to hang out with you? It was Rema, wasn't it? Look, I told you it was nothing."

"What are you mumbling about now?" Rema was at the door again with whispered tones that seemed odd for her.

"Nothing, it was nothing."

"Well, nothin' yourself on in the kitchen. The girls are almost finished and there's no tellin' when James will be boppin' down here."

"In a minute."

"Exactly, so come on. You know Kweku's flight gets in at eleven. Now you don't want him to find you *there,* do you?"

"Maybe."

"You better smile when you say that!"

Parker smiled broadly. "Be right there."

The Lessons of the Black Spy: The Deadly Con

An honest person cannot be conned. Only those who want something for nothing, only those who would fool others can be fooled.

Undoubtedly some agents were themselves conned. Those with transparent cover stories, those with too-well-pressed dashikis and too-short haircuts were probably easy marks. However, even when fingered, such an agent always had the metaphysics of spying working on his behalf: reality could be turned in on itself, any situation could be turned to advantage. The agent had simply to accuse his accuser.

When such accusations and counteraccusations were made, sometimes people died.

There are at least four major lessons offered by the activities of black agents:

1. Radical mass movements, as vehicles for the politics of protests, are untenable.

Because they could be so easily infiltrated, such movements, with a few notable exceptions, were decimated and/or manipulated.

2. A sense of the consequences of one's every action is essential.

Nothing with Rema, huh? Parker was in clear violation of Rollins's rule number two. She was quite a woman, that Rema. But Parker always felt as though she were playing with him, like when he asked her what Rollins had told her about him, she answered straight-up, "Not to trust you," elbowing Parker in the ribs.

The 1960s was a very dangerous period. Few blacks seem to have realized just how dangerous. Black agents were acutely aware. The agents and the organizations they represented saw themselves in a war situation with "dissidents." They acted accordingly.

3. Competence and skill are essential in any endeavor.

Because of their obvious intelligence and breadth of reading, agents were often given movement roles as theoreticians. Because of their obvious organizational abilities, agents were often appointed as movement chiefs of operations. And because of their skills in the martial arts and the use of firearms, and their considerable tactical abilities, agents were often made chiefs of security.

Other blacks involved in movement activities did not assume these responsible positions because they either were not as qualified or as assertive.

4. The only way to beat a con is to be of impeccable intent.

Maybe the only way to avoid being victimized by the con game was to assume the attitude of most of the blacks not involved in the liberation struggles of the 1960s: benign cynicism.

Maybe the "Activist Personality" lent itself to being conned. Maybe activists in their search for reinforcement and affirmation of their views set themselves up.

Maybe. Maybe Parker was a fat-ass after all. After all, he'd had to break a couple of arms to become security chief for that West Coast group. He also held several key committee positions, chairs and such, in three other organizations. But once his stations were secured, his SOP was to stand fast stonewall sit on it, to breed dissension and frustration, tie it up, bottle it up, all in the name of niggerdom, as in niggers ain't blank and niggers can't do blank, or failing that, to channel and monitor.

So much for the man of action. Maybe he *was* just another fat-ass with "a good government job."

Maybe. "Maybe Rollins should be our press agent—great copy. Mostly bullshit, but great copy. . . ."

Parker dozed, must have dozed off . . . heard screams, way off . . . down the hall . . . a dream perhaps . . . Rema running . . . running. . . .

Parker was back in the trees again, observing a body lying face down. It was him! "Am I dead?"

"If you want to be," the presence near Parker seemed to say. Was that Rollins?

"You mean I have a choice?" Parker glanced down again. There was a woman straddling the body.

"Maggie?"

"Ain't no Maggies here, man." Was that Willie?

"Mary Magdalen split when your Jesus Christ left." Yeah, that had to be Willie. "You did a mean J.C., man. I'm really gonna miss Him." That was Willie's chuckle alright.

Parker eyed the woman more closely. It was Doris. No, it was Rema. She either had her tongue in his ear, the way she sometimes did, or she was trying to rip the ear off with her teeth. Parker felt like a kid watching grownups "make love." It was frightening.

From his perch he could also see the hallway outside his room, where Rollins's bones seemed to be scattered. "Am I dead or what?"

"If you want to be. . . ."

The screams got louder, closer. . . .

Parker looked down again. No, it wasn't Rema at all. It was that nurse person, the one who was always staring at him through the glass. She was trying to lift him, turn him, roll him on his back. He'd rolled on his stomach, maybe dozed off. . . .

Splat! "Owww!" Parker's screams met Rema's at the head of the bed as she deposited the hot grits on the back of his right shoulder, wrist, and hand, which, lucky for him, was covering the side of his face. "What the—" Bam! She hit him in the mouth with the hot pot and leaped at him with a butcher knife. Parker rolled with her on the bed, fought her one-handed, still trying to shake and rub off those searing grits. They rolled to the floor. Cursing, crying, and scratching, Rema used everything Parker had taught her plus all that other stuff she already knew. And that other stuff had Parker bleeding. They struggled to their feet, her knee rising to his groin, his head butting her in the chin. She staggered back and he swung a half-assed right to her jaw out of his busted-nuts crouch. The blow sent Rema sprawling and Parker to his knees in pain. The sight and smell of the second- and third-degree burns on his hand and wrist made him feel faint. But he had no time for that. James would be coming.

Parker heard the girls already on the stairs calling, "James!" Soon they'd be banging on the kid's door. "That boy'll sleep right through the last day in time!" Willie had always said.

"No time to dress, the pants will be enough." Parker picked them out of the pile of clothes at the foot of the bed and pushed by Amina, who was standing in the doorway sobbing for her surrogate mother. As Parker stumbled past, she rushed to Rema, who sat dazed in the corner. Parker was in no shape for another fight—not with James. He had to get to his gun in the hall closet. What had Rema been screaming about? When he entered the hallway he knew.

"You won't be needin' them pants, sonny." Willie had Parker's gun, and he stood blocking the front door. Rollins wouldn't be coming home. He'd been shotgunned to death as he left the motel for the airport that morning. Janet had caught some of the pellets and had been hospitalized. Willie had just brought the news and now he was waiting for Parker. Willie knew who and what Parker was, and he figured Parker had set up the hit on Rollins.

"Come on, sonny." Willie seemed sober, but had tears in his eyes, "Come on."

Parker let go the pants and moved slowly toward the old man. He knew what James knew. He'd thought he knew what Rema knew. But he had no idea about Willie. World War I was a *long* time ago. And all the old man's stories about being a retired gangster seemed implausible. Gangsters don't draw Social Security. Do they?

Willie had picked his spot well, though, had the high ground, so to speak. But did he know enough to remove the safety? And his reflexes? Like rock growth probably? There was no way to maneuver in the narrow hall. Parker would have to talk his way in close enough for a juke fake and flying kick to the head.

. . . just like he gave Rollins. . . .

From his perch, Parker watched as the body, now in convulsions, was placed on a stretcher. The tremors shook Parker's tree. The thorazine had broken loose. The muscle contractions got progressively worse. The whole Forest shook as if in an earthquake. Parker couldn't hold on and was thrown from the treetops toward his body. He was certain he would enter it again but something repulsed him. It was like a cold. Willie had always said that colds were beings with two-week life spans that possessed, shared our bodies, and that our suffering provided the cold its opportunity for life. Yeah, Willie's nose ran a lot, especially when he was drinking.

It was running that morning. "Come on, son."

The basement door beneath the stairs was closer. But as Parker moved he saw that it was closed. Willie might even have locked it. Either way, Parker would have to hit it hard with a scalded shoulder to beat a bullet. Going over Willie seemed easier, if not more desirable. The next time he wiped his nose on his sleeve. . . . Rema was up yelling again for James, Willie, anybody to "Kill that nigger!"

The gun still at his side, Willie raised his other arm and began to wipe his nose. He took Parker's fake and creased the plaster of the wall high above and to the right of Parker's head. But the second shot caught Parker on his takeoff, ripped through his left cheek and earlobe, and sent him back head over heels. Parker landed flat on his face but was immediately lifted to his knees by the pain of the splinters, which dug deep into his hairline and forehead, when the third shot exploded the floor an inch from his head. Through his own blood, Parker watched as Willie drew nearer. He was *still* wiping his damned nose.

"Kill that nigger!" Rema was in the hallway.

"Poppa Willie?" That was James's voice. He was midway down the stairs, holding Janet's gun.

"Kill him!" Rema was inching down the hall with the butcher knife.

"Poppa Willie!" James's call went unanswered.

Willie had squared Parker up and was lost in the kill. He just kept humming something, some nontune, and shaking his head like an old blues singer about to hit the last chord.

Parker never heard the shot. All he noticed was the utter astonishment in Willie's eyes as the side of his head caved in.

"No!" Rema was on the run now, coming at Parker from behind. But before old Willie hit the floor, Parker had snatched the gun from his hand and fired three or four left-handed shots in James's general direction. One of them tore off the boy's kneecap and brought him tumbling head first down the stairs. Parker wasn't there to see him land. He was already in the vestibule fumbling with the front door and then he was gone.

Rema must have paused over Willie and James because Parker was halfway down the block before he heard her after him.

With both front doors open the wind whipped through the hallway and pushed open Rema's bedroom door. Amina, still huddled crying there in the corner, quickly rose to close it. It would be weeks, even after Janet returned, before Amina would venture into the hall again. As she slammed the door the backdraft kicked the edge of a bloody bedsheet from the page it covered:

The Legacy of the Black Spy: Few Conclusions

It was probably impossible to draw a *direct* cause-and-effect relationship between the pursuits of black agents in the 1960s and the inward-turning apathetic/anarchistic/materialistic/holy-rolling/drug-glut syndromes in black communities of the 1970s.

What can be said is that intelligence activities served to undercut existing charismatic black leadership and to undermine and stifle the emergence of future black leadership. Such activities also cut deeply into our sense of collective identity and common purpose, insidiously weakening those life-giving, life-sustaining functions of the group.

But perhaps the overriding legacy of the ubiquitous intelligence activities of the 1960s is a lingering suspicion. . . .

* * *

"Count on that crazy Ray Parker to be the first black streaker," someone remarked, oblivious to the blood and burns on Parker's body.

Someone else commented about how Parker never went anywhere without his gun—which was all he seemed to have on him at the time.

And folks really cracked up when they saw Rema chasing him with a butcher knife. Parker had to laugh too when he looked back and saw her with her headrag askew, bathrobe open, and one bedroom slipper, waving that blade and truckin', comin' on strong. He laughed at Rema, at himself, at "black *firsts*," laughed even though it hurt his face, then turned and ran on.

Folks disagree on what happened next. Some say that when Parker reached the highway, a block away, he shot out a tire, commandeered a car, and bumped on out of there on three wheels. Others say Parker was out of bullets and only waved a gun at passing motorists. But the junkies tell another story. They say Parker emptied his gun on tires, but despite some near collisions nobody, but nobody, would stop for a naked nigger with a gun—not in that part of town. The junkies say that when Rema closed on him, Parker picked his way across the highway, heading for the projects on the other side. They say he made it across, just barely, ran into the woods this side of the projects, with Rema in hot pursuit, but that he never came out.

Almost everybody agrees that they saw Rema walking back from the highway shivering. Somebody offered her a coat. She was still carrying that knife, but she also had Parker's gun.

FOURTEEN

Parker had to get to the woods. Back to the Forest. The doctors had finally discovered the cancer. It was spreading with such rapidity that various agencies were beginning to suspect one another of having administered "the treatment." Everyone, of course, denied it. Parker was a good man, a security risk in his present state, but a good man, nonetheless.

FIFTEEN

They say that at James's trial, Raynard Parker's name never came up. All testimony regarding him was disallowed. Parker's gun became Willie's gun. And the story the jury received was a child's story, the one Rosemary and Jamila told a sleepy James that February morning:

"Wake up! Mama says come quick!"

"What?"

"Hurry up! Everybody's downstairs fighting and Poppa Willie's got a gun!"

"What? Where?"

"Downstairs! Come on!"

They say that James was convicted of second-degree murder for killing Willie DuBois and given an indeterminate sentence which he is still serving, crippled leg and all.

They say that without Kweku's paychecks coming in, the Rollins household folded. Janet took her girls South to her parents' house. They say she finally pulled herself together and went on for her doctorate and now teaches at one of those black colleges.

Rema, they say, became a Bible-thumping evangelist, with Jamila singing and passing the plate. She moved initially into the storefront, which she converted into a "chapel," and now commands a congregation of over six hundred souls in a "real" church.

Having lost all her men in a single day, Rema found One more stable. And anyway, she always could rap.

It ain't evenin'——Al-mos' mornin'—It ain't

eve-nin'—Al-mos' mornin'—And the Lord done filled my

heart with song. It ain't eve-nin' Al-mos mor-nin'-It ain't

eve-nin'—Al-mos' mor-nin'

       It ain't evenin'   Almos' mornin'
       It ain't evenin'   Almos' mornin'
       And the Lord done filled my heart
           with song.
       It ain't evenin'   Almos' mornin'
       It ain't evenin'   Almos' mornin'

SIXTEEN

There is no lethal dosage of thorazine. The negative side effects determine the dosage. Parker's sandpaper tongue and constant, horizontal boogey suggested to the physicians that he'd had quite enough.

For about a week Parker floated in limbo. No matter how fast he ran, he couldn't reach the Forest. He had to get there somehow, so She could tell him what to do next. . . .

The only voice he heard now was Sieber's. Parker could have sworn he was back in the States.

SEVENTEEN

Maybe Rollins knew a few things about African thought, primitive reasoning patterns and such, like the importance of naming and names. But Parker wasn't sure Rollins really knew anything about Afro-Americans—Africans in America, as Rollins insisted on calling them. These "Africans," Parker retaliated, were as today's raisins in a bran-flakes box to the last century's grapes on the vine. "How long you say that box been on the shelf?" was Rollins's only reply.

It's true, they did laugh about the names thing: how a generation of Omares reduced to Omie would soon replace those Roosevelts reduced to Rosie; and how diminution to meaninglessness was really what this place was all about. But Parker wasn't sure about Rollins. Yeah, he did go on about blacks in the West ("Hey, the West is everywhere. It's on the Moon. It's whizzing past Jupiter, man!" Parker could not help himself). And how these blacks were of two minds.

"Two minds, my ass! We're two-headed freaks!" Parker wanted to be comical, to temper it somehow, but he couldn't. He could not even remember whether the conversation took place before or after Rollins was killed. All he could recall was his inability to coat it, to cover it and himself, to make it anything other than what it was:

A two-headed freak. He suddenly felt like a monster's mother—embarrassed, self-pitied, defiant, all that. But he could not stop.

"One of those heads is constantly expanding. Expanding so fast that it gets to be amorphous, like air. At one point you might have been able to pop it with a hatpin. But now, forget it. It's like 'the West.' To call this head 'white' is to stretch it to its limits—but then the 'whites' have always been the political extremists that the Druids and Gauls could never be.

"The other head is contracting so fast it's already like a Black

Hole, which is really neither a hole nor black. It's so concentrated, so closed in on itself, that it threatens to suck everything that exists right into it. But in the meantime, it constellates a whole bunch of world events about its core. And those events don't even know they're constellations." Parker was drenched with sweat, or was it blood?

Old Tommy Smirk laughed, really laughed; so Parker concluded it must be before, before and not after.

"Tell me, Ray," Rollins was game. "Tell me, should we now be relying less on our air head and more on our hole-in-the-head head? Or vice versa?"

Parker had never cracked a smile, and that's what finally broke Tommy Rollins up. He was quite literally on the floor.

"I told you it's not a hole at all, it's stuff so tightly packed, slave-ship packed, if you please, so turned back in on itself that it captures its own light. No, we don't need any more Maroon societies, New York's plenty."

Rollins whooped, actually cried out in the pain of laughter. He woke the children.

"Besides," Parker was oblivious to Rema's admonitions, and Rollins, with the edge of a throw pillow stuffed in his mouth and tears in his eyes, gestured frantically that she shouldn't interfere with Parker's roll.

"Besides, you get the same results with either head." Parker finally noticed the pillow, but he remained unruffled. "With the contracting head you get your hardcore blacks. Powerful. But their very tightness draws everything to them, including those things they've already outgrown and discarded—like their own shit and everybody else's shit—everything that's not nailed down. And since there's no way to nail down the nails, these niggers catch everything—acid indigestion, baby formula, big times, bright lights, booty-ooty-booga-mooga—you name it. All of it, everything anybody ever imagined. All the bucks and sewers stop right there."

"Now let me get this straight. These hardcores are the raisins in the bran flakes, right?" Rollins had dropped the pillow and was dragging himself back up on the sofa. "Then the 'air' must be the gas we get—and let—when we consume the box's contents?"

Parker ignored him. "With the expanding head you get niggers runnin' all over being trendy."

EIGHTEEN

Parker never learned who authorized or if there was any authorization for the Rollins hit. Everybody denied it, even the young man who was ultimately convicted for it.

Yes, that spy piece was risky, stupid even. That's it, stupid, student-stupid. Rollins had been hanging out with students for too long. Rollins and Parker had disagreed about the students' rights to stupidity. They finally agreed that faulty premises and fanatical conclusions were certainly a part of the school experience, issued like gym shorts. But not everybody took gym.

NINETEEN

They say that about a year before his death, Rollins approached Rema about "fixing" a dream. Rema had spoken of it before: how to alter the outcome of a prophetic nocturnal message.

Rollins had dreamed of his own death by gunfire, watched a man whom he knew pull the trigger, felt his own body, stiff and then limp, fall away, off to one side, continued to witness undiminished as the killer wiped a tear and ejected the spent casing onto the human shell.

Rollins told Rema about the setting: a church with pews which kept becoming a bookstore with shelves, as dreams will do, described the people present, all except the assailant. That he'd fix—along with the outcome. . . .

Circumstances would suggest that his success was limited.

T W E N T Y

They say it was the day before he was killed. That day when Rollins read the title of his paper at his first and final presentation up at State College, a whole contingent of nationalists got up and walked out. Ray Parker would have been proud. Hot Damn! Just the title! Of course, Rollins, as usual, had added the words "of the 1960s" after "and Other Male Fantasies." Perhaps he thought that addition would distance it sufficiently. However, everybody knew Kweku spoke only on current events, the eternal now he wanted folks to overcome.

By the time Rollins reached the meat of the paper, another group of nationalists had left, these muttering variations on Rollins's given name aloud. And even the moderate blacks were beginning to squirm. They were both embarrassed by the nationalists' display and confused by Rollins's talk. After all, they *had* sided with these "militants" in an unprecedented joint endorsement of Rollins for the newly vacant Director of Minority Affairs/Chair of Ethnic Studies position. And this *was* the first time a black had spoken at State's convocation. That African communist back in '59 didn't count.

They say that the this-is-*our*-boy broad smiles on the faces of State's Prez and Dean and the rapt attention and applause from the predominantly white audience was just a bit much for the nationalists. Too bad. It was probably the shortest, most subtle convocation speech in the college's history. And most of the subtlety was lost on the whites: " . . . every black organization, project, or curriculum should be divided into age grades with separate generational priorities, agendas, outlets for socializing, and griots." " . . . it's only been a few years since he was assassinated, but already black undergraduates are referring to him as 'Malcolm the Tenth,' as though he were some long-lost monarch.

"Every generation claims *its* time as the most crucial, the most profound and/or the worst. And every generation is right. Today's undergrads, our students, have no sense of those times which have made us what we are. They have no sense of it because they were too young. They had not yet, as the Gullahs say, 'caught sense.' Our task is to somehow help our students catch and make sense of *these* times." In his only gesture, Rollins extended his right arm with his index finger pointed at the floor. "We can only do that by directly confronting our own fantasies."

Rollins paused respectfully as more blacks left the hall. They say he smiled at a woman named Janet seated in the front row. He might have even anticipated seeing Ray there too. But Rollins probably knew where Ray would be. How could he not know? Rema had never been more radiantly Rema.

"Fantasies are the result of needs. What needs? And why male fantasies?"

When Parker saw that line—yes, he'd secretly scanned a copy of the speech long before it was delivered, just as he'd read every letter written or received, every note, scratch, or doodle from Rollins's hand, everything in the house except that goddamned dream journal Janet always carried with her. Reading Kweku's stuff was Parker's job and his passion—anyway, that line flashed Ray back to something Doc had said:

"Men don't exist in nature. They're anomalies, human inventions. The only natural humans are women. Women are born. Men are always created by other men who steal bits and pieces of behavior normal for women, like bloodletting, and blow it out of proportion, distort it into elaborate rituals. . . ."

TWENTY-ONE

Was that Sieber's voice? "Mr. Parker, can you hear me? It's Jake. Can you hear me? Hey, can you hear me?"

"Yeah, I can hear you." Parker was descending from the fog.

So much for the doctor/client confidentiality pact. Sieber was there. Had he always been on the government's payroll? Had he just been called in? No matter. He was there at Parker's bedside. There, leaning over him.

Parker made a quick move but the restraints held him fast. Sieber jumped in his chair, obviously startled. The intern moved to Parker and gently pressed his shoulders back against the sheets.

Ah, Miss Gruber, I don't think the restraints will be necessary now." Sieber had regained his composure.

Parker watched her hands as she removed the arm straps. Her fingers were long and slender, unlike someone's he could recall. Marcie? No, Macy.

Her name was Macy. Her first name. Parker had laughed knee-bent and thigh-slapped when he heard it and asked if her mother had been frightened during pregnancy by a very large balloon.

"No. And I wasn't born in November!" was her reply. Then they both smiled at each other.

When Doris found out about Macy she walked. Up and out in a day. First to a motel, then to her own apartment. The whole move was accomplished in less than a month. Gone.

Parker couldn't understand it. Hell, he and Macy only did those things that Doris had no interest in. Like skydiving and disco discourse, you know, shouting back and forth to the beat, and well, yeah, they had done some other things too.

He'd met her when she was still an undergrad. It was in a laundromat, where she was complaining as only the wealthy can about the number of coins she had to invest in her wash. Parker had, of course, disagreed, but soon conceded that while she had many, he, like most men, had only one load. They smiled at each other again.

But those fingers . . . Macy had stubby fingers, "Piaf fingers," Parker called them. He had a whole theory worked out about those kinds of fingers—too short, they made a person grabby. Their owners never seemed to get enough. Kinky fingers. After Doris, he held a lot of hands.

Parker was staring at the intern's hands and her slender fingers. He then sought her face: "Maggie?"

"No, Margaret." Great bedside mannerisms, lilting voice and all.

"I didn't think so." He smiled at her through parched lips. Then Parker hauled off and punched Sieber in the eye.

Parker was hustled back to his cell, where he promptly assumed his old position at the center of the space. He could feel the intern's and Sieber's eyes on the back of his neck. He ignored the muffled conversation in the hallway and listened instead for his own voices. They were still absent.

Parker sat there on the floor and looked about. Rollins's bones still lay scattered in the corner to Parker's right and in the hallway beyond. The Forest still loomed before him. He sat motionlessly, knowing the watchers could not match his patience. He waited until they left his window. Then he rose and silently entered the Forest.

TWENTY-TWO

"Whore!" the young construction worker muttered as he brushed by Parker and Macy on the narrow street. Parker's Arabic was minimal but he understood *that* word. He immediately stopped and turned to stare at the young paper hat and his older companion. The Stateside hard hats would have known better. They would have said it, but not out loud. No, they, even through a beer haze-glaze, would have seen death in Ray's eyes and in his walk. That would have made them cautious. But not the Arabs, or the French for that matter. These seemed to court death just like the two who now returned Parker's glare.

Macy smiled nervously as she gently tugged at Ray's arm. The Arabs were still smiling, so she figured there was still a chance. Although she had lived on the Riviera for a year, Macy had yet to venture this way. The Rue Obscure was aptly named. Arched and dark, it offered too many passageways for retaliation. Only with Ray and at his insistence had she come—but they would leave at hers.

She goosed him! Took her hand and ran it vigorously up and down the crack of his ass, rudely tried to penetrate the fabric of his slacks.

Parker jumped literally a couple of feet in the air then quicksilver turned to knock Macy's hand away.

"Whose side you on?"

Eye contact broken, the confrontation was over. The Arabs were laughing, slapping dusty shoulders, and continuing on their way. Parker was left in their dust and derisive laughter.

Humiliated, he spoke to Macy the way he had the day before, pimp-style, low and angry. Then he gripped her about the waist and practically dragged her toward the light at the end of the street.

Small wonder folks mistook the nature of their relationship. Perhaps the Arabs were not to be faulted nor was that would-be hero, the old Frenchman from the day before. The Frenchie had stood just five feet down the rail, held his ground against Ray's evil eye, and waited for any sign from Macy for assistance. And through her tears Macy had acknowledged the old gentleman's presence. She was truly grateful for his unselfish concern, for any man's unselfish concern.

"Damned hero," Ray had shouted at the Frog, and he would have killed the old man and tossed him over the rail into the Mediterranean had he interfered. Or at least Parker would have tried. Something, it was still intangible, but something about all these old guys had become less predictable of late.

Though she was deeply hurt, Macy managed a smile and nod at the Frenchman as Parker rushed her away. Appropriately, the source of Macy's pain was Ray's vicious attack on what he termed her "whore's-eye view" of love and marriage.

"Look, babe, among folks who sleep around as much as you and me there is always this foolish notion of the nocturnal visitor who will swoop down—swing-low sweet anybody—steal in, and rescue us from our cycle of, how you say it in French, *pointless encounters,*" Ray gave it his foppish best. And then, turning the knife, "It's prime this way, with you here and me coming in two, three times a year. Just be sure not to schedule me the same time as the fleet!"

As Macy's tears welled up again, Parker pulled her to him. Quickly overcoming her resistance, he played her like a harp. It was really too easy. With her, even the Maginot Line held.

Parker could have written a textbook on such women, with color-coded workbooks. Fathers seemed to be the key. Either dad was too distant, arms folded, no arms, away forever—or too friendly, with big hands rammed down little panties, or too angry, with big fists slammed into small faces.

Parker had a keen eye for their scars. Desperation seemed to be their common bond. Promiscuity their path. The ones with the ripped panties seemed more likely to sell the booty. The others usually gave it away. None of them was so much oversexed as underloved. And any semblance of love would do, from a serious ass-kicking to—Oh, Lord, don't send them flowers!

Each met flowers with some skepticism: from "No, no, not for me?" to "What d'ya think this gonna get ya, chump?"

Ray concluded that the sincerity of delivery was crucial: If you take the rough route with the pappy-fucked, you have to convince her that you care enough to put her permanently out of her misery. And if you're reckless enough to take the flower route with *those* bitches, you better be good at playing off her desire to scam you like any other Dick against her silent hope that you and Prince Charming own the same horse. Any pimp worth his fascination for this type knows how to mix the hard with the soft horse manure.

With the others, the neglected and the battered, you play them by ear, but always play them. Hey, the sex is fantastic, if a bit sad and sticky. And never take their sob stories seriously. Oh, they're "true" alright. But at a dime apiece they could sustain Xerox to the millennium. Just keep scratching out and replacing the woman's name at the top.

Parker had almost mistaken Macy for someone special. It was probably her look. Dark curly hair, green eyes, freckles. Others often made similar mistakes. The Israelis could have sworn she was *the* American Princess. To the French she was *super chouette*. For the Arabs she had a look that only the veil could redeem. And Brazilians with their mulatto songs would have been very confused, indeed.

But Doris called it straight out the box and put it into perspective for Ray: "White bitch!!"

Ah, yes, the color thing. Workbook A: The best white broads are the ones you don't know. All the others' feet stink. He'd have to speak to that nurse when he got back. Back? He bet *her* feet didn't stink. . . .

With black women it was a whole 'nother thing, according to

Willie. "You've heard it before: 'It's hard to impress 'em.' That's 'cause most of 'em have scoped the *back* of the billboard, where *all* is revealed."

Well, okay, Macy's physical appearance *did* pose a few problems for Ray's work. He'd certainly whipped the melanic maneuver on enough folks to know its effectiveness. Macy would definitely have to remain his far-out-of-town woman.

It was her sparkle, her openness, he admired, or so he said. He was even annoyed to learn that she was "into black guys" like she might have been "into" macrobiotic cooking or jogging. But her willingness to accommodate his whims was extremely ingratiating. How many abortions had there been?

No, it wasn't skin. Nothing was that simple anymore. Parker just had no use for the dark side of the moon. He was strictly a sunshine man. Doris had taught him that. He tended to disappear at the approach of her dark moods.

Of course Willie had picked up on it: "Sheba can lounge in Ray's bed all day, but Kali had better not show *her* black ass!"

* * *

Rema was different. Some other order of being? Not really. But certainly not a type Parker would have known, as they say, "socially," that is, outside of his work. There was no desperation in her. She, however, had immediately sensed his. She never used it against him, although she certainly could have. And Parker never thought she would. That wasn't her way.

Rema was like those trees near the village, the kind that are drums in the making, concerned with giving shape to the sounds which would resonate through the generations.

"Now don't get me wrong! It's not any of that hokey Mother Africa stuff, man." Parker was leaving Sieber's office for a meeting across the Bay.

"This woman ain't strong, she ain't weak. But she's got an incredible sense of home." Then, closing the door and half to himself,

"Maybe these times let some of them be what they already are, but without the bullshit. . . ."

* * *

Different but not perfect. What had she done? Oh, yeah, the hair thing. For the minute, or year, Africanoid features were fashionable, Rema had worn a rag on her head. She suddenly saw her semi-straight hair and pale skin as pollutions. In the same minute, or was it really a year, dark, demure Janet blossomed. She discarded her wigs and actually sunbathed! Miracle year that.

Rollins had tried to explain the hair thing to him, but Parker never really understood. To Parker it had to be self-hatred of the most profound sort: that black women wouldn't, no, couldn't go out of doors with the gods-given stuff on top of their heads as the gods had given it. Combs and brushes weren't even the issue, and "fashion" was a blind.

"We're talkin' lye and grease here, man—and FIRE!" Parker shouted. "And it ain't like they've lost the art of plaiting, 'cause every little girl's got her braids with bright ribbons and roadmap parts!"

"Fire, that's right, fire," Rollins had begun softly and slowly. "Beauticians are the mistresses of fire, hot-comb-and-curler smiths," his delivery was cadenced as though he spoke from the dead, "alchemists: coarse to fine, nappy to straight, initiate girls in woman flames. . . ."

Parker snapped his fingers to break the spell. "Hey, then give me *girls!*"

TWENTY-THREE

February is . . . a second-class month, alive with second-class cravings and craziness . . . the lull between fiery birth and blustery return . . . a place to get gassed up between New Year's Eve and spring . . . the New Jersey-Delaware of months, shortchanged, leap-yeared, and marginal . . . the nigger month.

In the summer, the Forest is always cooler. Winter is something else again. Numb feet and sweaty brow.

The woods drop away moving toward the waters, those streams that run winding in their midst. Down run whether you want to or not down run or fall and roll fall stumble away . . . toward the chthonic convulsions . . . toward Her.

Always demons at the gate, ourselves unmastered as yet unmasked stumbling selves unrealized. Shock at their coming—and ours. Shame of discovery. Ignore them/know them then get on with it on to the stream on to the silent gurgle arrogant in its silence awful in its silence . . .

. . . warm inside the White, surprisingly warm 98.6 radiating back on itself again and again, double-yoke warm, boiling itself or hatching itself.

Perhaps white-hot grits flung at a black face is Geronimo's revenge for the Ninth Cavalry. What had been used before? Flaming fufu mixed with palm oil? It must, after all, cling like snow to a sweaty brow while it burns.

* * *

Parker stumbled on the moist decay of leaves his feet could no longer feel. Snow was falling again, more heavily than earlier in the day. The Forest incline was less steep now but more slick, as though deliberately sliding him toward its center. Those zombies he'd encountered at the edge were not pursuing him, as he'd suspected, nor was the woman. Fleeing from a woman? He could have turned at any point and blown her away. But he hadn't, even when she joined the zombies. Why not? He didn't know. He knew only that he had to plunge his throbbing wrist beneath the stream's frozen run.

He blankly observed his own knees as they came up below him in slow motion, one after another. Boney knees. Knees to remember like those of that old Arab who would hike up his wachamacallit and run like crazy when the pipe bomb exploded just seconds after ardent admirers had whisked the unholy man from his car. Such running for a seventy-year-old! In extreme fear or nearness to death, feets-don't-fail-me-now never touch the ground. Parker couldn't tell the difference anymore: flyin' or dyin'?

Anyway, that pipe-bomb caper was really getting raggedy. Come on now, how many times can you clock-and-pressure-rig the passenger seat on a Volks and claim the occupants were transporting explosives? Just 'cause it worked in B'more didn't mean they had to use it again in Guyana, and it would already be too late in Iran— like everything else there. What did they think? That people were stupid? That they never read newspapers? Newspapers?!

When the embassy broke, Parker would assume the young rads were coming for him with that old Arab up front leading the way. Could Ray's ego endure yet another blow? Could be nobody "reads."

* * *

Parker watched the woman move toward him with strides of such confidence that he almost gave ground. It was Doris.

"You act as though you don't know me." Parker's words and body reached for her with an erection.

"Does anyone?" She was annoyed with him, impatient. "Do you know *me?* Do you even care to know about me? You never ask me about *my* work. You don't want to hear about *my* feelings."

"Maybe I know too much already, about too many people and too many feelings."

"Now what's *that* supposed to mean?" She was backing away from him now, avoiding his touch.

"Hey, babe. I come here to unwind. . . ."

"Unwind? You mean to hide!"

"If you prefer. . . ."

"I don't!"

She moved away as swiftly as she had come. And Parker was alone.

"Look, when they want you, they get you, even if they gotta level the whole Forest just to uncover your particular rock. I ain't lyin'. Ask the gooks. Ask Nat," Ray mumbled to the treetops.

* * *

As he moved along, Parker absentmindedly fingered the keloid around an old shoulder wound. It was his left shoulder, the old Hopalong Cassidy–Gene Autry–Roy Rogers-fix-upfix-up-let's-play-again-Saturday shoulder, with its bullet hole of the week. He remembered how Doris was almost glad when he first got shot—after she was certain he wasn't dead. The wound insured them at least six months' recovery time together.

He remembered practicing his sleeping act on Doris: how he pretended to be asleep with his head on her lap and how she took liberties with his body that he never would have allowed were he "awake." He did need the practice. It came in handy. He sometimes heard important, whispered conversations that way.

But as Doris's hands moved lightly over his bare chest and shoulders and finally caressed his face, Parker bolted upright, startling even himself. Hadn't he told her *never* to touch him while he slept? He'd told her that. But maybe Doris knew when he was only pretending. Maybe Rollins wasn't just breezin'. Maybe everyone knew.

* * *

He hadn't realized that he'd fallen nor did he know how long he'd lain there on his side with the snow gently covering him. He could not feel his legs and arms, but these seemed respectively to be drawn up and wrapped about him. And Her hands were on him, Her breath in his ear as She whispered secrets. Parker was warmed by Her presence as by the white blanket. And they made love or so he thought and their rhythms were those of the silent stream.

The secrets were things he always knew, such simple things like first light.

TWENTY-FOUR

The next thing Parker knew, he stood there in the hallway outside his padded room, one hand held fast by the wall. He jerked his hand and understood in an instant that the wall was in as much pain as he. The wall moaned with him and bled as he bled. He caressed the wall and was himself soothed. . . .

He stroked Her and sang what seemed to be musical equations to Her and the wall in Amharic, Yoruba, Mayan, Chinese, Gaelic, and Greek. He then proceeded to call each particle of the wall by name, as She trembled.

Parker wasn't sure how long the intern had been standing there watching him. But she didn't seem the least bit frightened by his predicament. She extended her hand.

"May I help you, Mr. Parker?"

"Maggie?"

"No, Margaret."

"Close."

"Margaret Gruber. Margaret Gruber," she repeated hesitantly as if trying to remember something. Then finally: "May I be of assistance, Mr. Parker?" She extended both her hands, her eyes fixed on his. Parker's eyes were alive again. His face had returned.

"Venus in . . ." he led.

"Pisces," she answered without any conscious knowledge or belief in such things.

"Mars in . . .?"

"Cancer (really?)" she thought to herself.

"Close enough," Parker sang in quiet falsetto slowly extending his right hand to her and placing it softly between hers. Something came and something or nothing went. Birth and death rejoiced in a song of light. And the light was everywhere. And the light was blackness fused with light.

* * *

The explosion was heard throughout the complex. Guards were on the scene in an instant. Fire control units were en route. What they found has remained under a Top Secret classification to this day.

The composite scuttlebutt that always manages to seep out from under such classifications gave the following account: There was this explosion down in the loony ward that somehow pulverized one of the walls of a padded cell. The cinder block outer wall was reduced to heaps of fine white dust. The padding material was so rarified as to be undetectable, except by sophisticated instruments used to determine the presence of certain elements in the air. The "poison gas" which apparently killed the first two guards to enter the hall was that polyurethane cloud from the padding.

This crazy nigger who had been confined to that particular cell was found an hour or so later after that part of the complex had been cleared and gas masks issued. He was found in the hallway outside his cell under the largest mound of that dust. It was soon determined that the mound was so large because there were two people under it: this nigger and a white woman, a nurse, underneath him.

Now the fact that this nigger and white lady were butt naked might have been cause for an instant riot had not the soldiers who made the find been black and, and hence, supposedly more tolerant of such couplings. It was rumored that all the searchers were black because the shapes of their heads better suited the gas masks. And, anyway, the first two unfortunate guards *were* white. . . .

Everyone assumed that the dust-covered pair was dead because of the absence of breath. However, a slight pulse was soon detected in each, so the nigger and the lady were rushed to intensive care.

Nobody knows how the nigger beat the rape charge (reduced from rape and attempted murder). Probably pleaded insanity.

Some say that what never reached the scuttlebutt was the extensiveness of the tests conducted on that white dust. And only a few at the Pentagon are said to have known of the conclusions reached:

that virtually every cell of the cinder blocks' structure was exploded from the inside; that, although considerable light and sound were emitted, there was no heat; that the other inevitable radiations emitted remained unknown; and that the only apparent results of the exposure to these unknown radiations was the complete loss of the male's body hair and the discoloration of the female intern's skin and hair. The couple's garments were never found. Oh, yes, there was one other curiosity. The male had somehow lost his left hand. There was no wound, no blood, no evidence of a wound having been cauterized. The nub of the wrist was seamless, completely smooth as though no hand had ever been there attached.

They say that further tests revealed that Parker had also lost his cancer. Moreover, he seemed to have undergone a profound personality transformation. He wasn't exactly rational, but he *had* apparently stopped hallucinating.

A white-haired, dark-skinned Margaret Gruber, on the other hand, babbled on about a "vision" (Was that really Parker in the hall?), about a touch, and about a light.

Everybody wanted to know what happened to their clothes. Parker's only reply was that babies always get dressed *after* a birth.

TWENTY-FIVE

Willie might have said of Margaret's new appearance: "The minstrels have been redeemed, the black face restored to its esteemed pedestal. Puttin' on the black face is a *sacred* thing again. Hey, the black one is back!"

They say that Margaret's parents came almost immediately to sign their daughter out of the hospital. It seems she had told them enough about the institution's procedures that the Grubers didn't want their little girl subjected to anymore "tests." After a big stink that lasted for about a week, Margaret was released to her parents with the stipulation that she see one of the private physicians on the approval list pinned to her shirt front.

They say that Margaret disappeared shortly thereafter, much to the dismay of everyone involved. The Grubers charged the hospital with kidnapping. The hospital charged the Grubers with libel and slander. But no one ever saw her again.

Of course, there are those rumors about the itinerant healer who seems to match Margaret's description and who to this day continues to move freely through the rural areas of Western and Eastern Europe curing the infirm with a touch.

TWENTY-SIX

Parker met with Sieber and two other "doctors" every day for a week in what crudely resembled a debriefing session.

Parker focused on Sieber and told him everything. He even gave him the cure for cancer and in terms he figured Sieber could understand:

"You know the Kabala?"

Sieber nodded affirmatively.

"Well, when we fail to acknowledge and honor the host, gods, if you like, when we fail to cultivate the Tree of Life, then the Tree's energies are choked and they back up in us, run amok in us." Parker paused deliberately, watching as one of Sieber's associates, shaking his head, slowly pulled out his prescription pad. He, at least, must have really been a doctor.

Sieber, annoyed, immediately dismissed the two men. The real doctor apologized and left. The other man protested vehemently about an "agreement" and national security and such. With some difficulty Sieber persuaded him to leave. Then with a sweeping gesture of assurance he switched off the tape recorder, smiling at Parker.

Parker returned the smile: "Look, Doc, we both know this room is bugged!"

They laughed, took a brief break and then continued.

"Tell me again about the Wall."

"I told you, I was finger-fuckin' this Woman—"

"The nurse?"

"No. Well, yes and no. No. No, not really."

"With your left or right hand?"

Parker held up the nub in mute reply. He had done this in answer to several of Sieber's questions, enough times, in fact, to piss the good doctor right off:

"Now you stop giving me that goddamned fingerless finger when I ask you something."

Parker patiently replied that the "finger" that people "give" to one another in hostility and in hostile jest is really the sign of the most sacred of measurements:

"From the tip of the elbow to the tip of the longest finger is a *cubit*. You might say I took the measure of that Woman and she of me. Yeah, I finger-fucked her, talked shit to her, and she came. And when she came she took my left hand as a trophy and as a tribute to our union." Parker caressed the nub.

Sieber was becoming increasingly agitated and aggravated: "Hey, look, don't talk shit to *me!*"

"Shit's a very powerful substance," Parker was calm, "a medium for growth. There is no waste, only the means for transformations. Shit's the best example for that. I'm being *serious* with you," he assured Sieber, "that's why I'm using your own power words."

"Okay, what happened to that wall?" Sieber took a long breath, shaking his head and loosening his tie.

"I don't really know. You'll have to ask the left hand. It obviously found out a lot, probably what the daisy and the bees knew right away. Maybe that hand learned more than I could ever assimilate and that's why She wouldn't give it back to me."

"Well, you've obviously undergone a traumatic experience. However, more talk like that has got to make you a candidate for—"

Before Sieber could finish his thought, Parker was in his face. It wasn't a glare. There was no threat, no anger, in Parker's eyes nor in his words. He said simply: "No drugs." But the words rang with a finality of "It is done" or "So be it" from the voice of the prophets of old or that old black deacon's simple "Amen."

Sieber was transfixed as Parker assumed his seat. The doctor finally heard himself muttering: "Tell me, ah, Ray, tell me again about ah, tell me about what you learned in your 'Forest.'"

"I can't remember."

"Try!"

"I can only remember a few lines—but I can't seem to recall the key. . . ."

TWENTY-SEVEN

They say that Parker began to sing. At first there were no words, only notes, several octaves, an incredible range, high and low, just notes. The first run cracked the walls and took out the entire audio monitoring system. Only later would Sieber notice the blood trickling from his own ears. Sieber would also later discover that Parker had had no previous musical skills. But in that instance the doctor merely assumed that all black people . . . well, you know.

Then the words came. In free verse the story of the Forest sojourn. Parker recited or sang (it was actually both at once) for seventy-two hours, nonstop. Sieber took furious notes, at first, but then discovered that most of what Parker was saying was gibberish, as though there were not yet words for what he was trying to express so he would interject pure sound, often high pitched. Some of it even seemed to be glossolalia. With a failed technology, Sieber resorted to rotating stenographers, who took down as much as they could.

On the second day, Sieber brought in a musicologist, whose tape recorder was soon rendered inoperative by Parker's vocal gymnastics. After being assured that his equipment would be replaced, the musicologist agreed to do a written notation on Parker.

Early on the morning of the third day, as Sieber sat dozing in a chair, it came to him, as they say, in a dream. He suddenly knew what Parker was doing: interspersed with his own experiences, Parker was relating the entire organic history of the Forest. The "music" was the collective tonal equivalency of the continuing process of creation itself.

In the dream Sieber awoke to find his goatee was now a full Hasidic beard and his bald spot was flourishing with new growth that curled about his shoulders. Sieber blinked and found himself actually staring into a cracked mirror. He turned to find that the musicologist had left and that the latest stenographer had assumed a fetal postion on the sofa. Sieber tried to wake her, to no avail. He tried to telephone her replacement, but now the phones were dead.

"Damn you, Parker!" Sieber glared at his patient, who still sat there as before, singing.

The guard in the hallway was genuinely startled by Sieber's appearance. He insisted on inspecting the doctor's identity card before complying with Sieber's request for more coffee and a fresh stenographer.

When the doctor reentered the room, the song was completed and Parker was gone. The guards searched the entire complex several times but found no trace of him. It was as if he had passed undetected through concrete and steel.

TWENTY-EIGHT

They say the Army was even more interested in Parker then. His superiors, of course, wanted to replicate his "trick." Their specialists poured over the scraps of audio tape, transcripts, and musical notations for months. They also tried to account for the phenomenal growth of the plants in the room where Parker was interrogated and for Sieber's new head of hair. And why didn't Parker's hair grow? Couldn't he hear what he was saying?

Sieber never did reveal his dream to the authorities. Some say he was actually afraid that he was still dreaming, that all his encounters with Parker had been dreams. Sieber did admit to his friends a few years later that he still had conversations with Ray during what Sieber called waking dreams.

"You mean hallucinations?" countered Sieber's friends.

"No, those things aren't real. These are different. Real. You see?"

"Ah, yes we do." Poor Jake.

* * *

Rachael Sieber signed the commitment papers herself. Jake Sieber wasn't the first white or quasi white to be nigger-possessed. And he probably would not be the last.

But before they put Sieber away, he wrote down the content of those conversations and what he had gleaned from Parker's three-day solo performance.

TWENTY-NINE

Strange spirits inhabit Manhattan. Aggressive, crafty, and strident. The local "Indians" knew them personally and were amused but mainly frightened by them. How could creatures be so relentless, so driven? The locals were predictably relieved and pleased to divest themselves of such an evil place.

Now poppies were relative newcomers to the isle. But they immediately fell into the overriding competitive vibration. In fact, the poppies were soon able to overcome the violent majority spirits by transporting the poppies' commiserates back to those pristine ancestral fields of their common births. It was truly a symbiotic relationship, for the consciousness of the human devotees always returned the favor. The poppies attracted both the swift and the slow, but always those who bucked the prevailing "winds." (Everyone knows that "wind" is simply the effect of the counterclockwise motion of beings unseen.)

Then something peculiar happened. Many poppies suddenly found themselves keeping company with dry, stiff mud. Or was it clay? No matter. This once moist substance had only one experience to relate to the poppies. The Fire. The glorious, transforming flame. Like most religious converts, these "bricks," as they were appropriately called, were a bore with their babble.

Just as suddenly, other poppies found themselves among moist, rooted but somewhat resistant beings. While these beings knew nothing of the flame, they were nonetheless too busy with their upward striving, their lofty aspirations, to regard the self-indulgent poppies as anything other than irritants. And the poppies weren't too pleased with being ignored.

Even on *that* island these were not commonplace occurrences. . . .

THIRTY

They say that one day in Berkeley, Parker came upon a copy of Sieber's book *The Peter Pan Chronicles,* which had been published shortly after the doctor's unfortunate death. The book had been at the top of the bestseller list since its release.

It was all there in the first person singular, almost everything Parker had told him, with nary a footnote nor citation. All Sieber.

"Plato lives," Parker read from the review excerpt reprinted on the book jacket, as he placed it back on the shelf.

They say that Parker clapped his hands and laughed out loud.

THIRTY-ONE

That's right, *hands*.

They say that Jake Sieber knew about Parker's new left hand. Knew about it and wrote about it, but that it was one of those "absurdities" which Rachael Sieber, as self-appointed editor, had carefully excised. Actually, Rachael did a brilliant editing job and truly deserved all those royalties and talk-show appearances.

Anyway, according to those who scanned the epic in its original, massive, and seemingly incoherent form, when Parker left Germany he went to New York, where he set about the mission of restoring all the junkies to health. Of course the major drug dealers were not pleased and most of the junkies were uncooperative and even downright hostile. There were, however, a few highly evolved junkies, musicians mainly, who opted for the cure. The cure required the patient, assisted by certain incantations, to pass through a brick wall. Parker's speciality was really cinder block but there seemed to be more brick walls in New York than anything else. The object was to imprison the self-possessed spirit of the poppies inside the cells of the brick.

Parker was quite successful with those few who persevered. And it still seems strange that the drug dealers' hitmen could never find Parker. After all, how many bald-headed, one-handed men are there in Harlem? Certainly not more than a couple of dozen.

Unfortunately, one of Parker's disciples, a bass player named Carlton, perverted the techniques. Carlton soon had junkies passing through tree trunks—because it was easier and faster. One of Carlton's followers, a person of ambiguous gender known only as "the Kid," wound up selling secret incantations (at least those mispronounced fragments which had filtered down) to second-story men. Most of these unfortunate people suffered horrible deaths, as they were able to pass only partially through the walls of buildings they sought to burglarize. The Kid eventually met a similar fate: encased in cement at the bottom of the East River.

By the time New York's Finest launched an investigation, Parker had already been brought up on charges by those trees Carlton had violated.

Parker found himself again in the Forest, for a trial. Found guilty, he grew a new left hand as punishment for providing the left-hand path another outlet in this world and as a reward of restoration for the same deed.

THIRTY-TWO

In the Forest: first or second time? Or was this the third time? Impossible to tell. Time does not exist in the Forest....

In the Forest, Parker experienced his whole life from before conception to after his death, but without sequence.

There he was hovering over the bed with what seemed like innumerable beings all watching the attractive couple rocking, jazzing, rolling, and doing all those other musical things together. The beat was incredible, lights flashed, Macy pressed against him, hard, as the other couples on the floor gave ground. "Do it, do it!" "Partee!" Parker was about to ejaculate when he noticed the indifference on the faces of the other men in the darkened theater, where only the prurient glow of the screen gave light. Indifference or veiled leers? He wondered if they too were there to seek birth or to learn to avoid it.

Attractive indeed! The couple's strokes were pulling Parker in. "Make it last!" "Not now, not now!" "Oh, Lord!" Joe Parker shuddered and heaved. Emma Jones Parker winced. But Ray-Parker-to-be saw it too late, her expression and its meaning: boredom, disgust, and pain. Too late. He was in, up in there! Warm. Like his mother's bed, like Rema's bed, like the Forest floor, like his own blood spurting like semen from his wrist.... More like that: warm and moist.

* * *

But now he was cold. The wind was seeping into his bones.

It was awfully cold, much too cold, too many days in a row for late August. But the children played on as they had the entire summer. Many were shirtless, all were dirty. They made a terrible racket. And that young woman was out there again too: their mother, older sister? The dust rose as the children scurried about, all nine or so of them, just out of the woman's reach. Above their throng of squeals, her curses rode harsh and wide as she swatted at them. She seemed to be addressing the sky and every being thereunder. She was, of course, ignored, except by the small girl who sat on the slanted roof high above the rest.

Parker sat on Rollins's porch again, watching the children. Directly across from Rollins's house was a vacant lot through which Parker could see the back of the row house over on the next block. He watched the children there as he had daily. As usual he was also trying to talk to Rema, listen to Rema, but as usual all he could hear was that other woman's voice. He was about to turn his back on her, the children, and Rema, and wait for Tommy Smirk inside the house, where it might be quieter and warmer, when he spotted the girl on the roof.

"How the hell did she ever get up there?" Parker thought out loud.

"Who?"

He was pointing her out to Rema when the little girl got up, her perch shattered by the woman's shout. As she rose, the girl's bare feet slid toward the roof's edge. She tried to stand as she went, and was erect when she began her three-story drop.

As the girl fell, Parker was already up and running across the street, then across the lot. Rema was close behind him, gaining on him. Damn, she was fast. Too fast. . . .

The children scattered as though *they* had done something wrong. The little girl lay crumpled on the ground, but her limbs strained to flee with the others.

Parker loped to a halt and pushed the woman aside. She had been standing there screaming at the girl to get up, and now she screamed at Parker to "Get the hell out of my yard!"

Parker pushed her again. "Go get some blankets!"

"Get out of here!" The woman raised her fist.

"Go get the fuckin' blankets!" Parker was nose to forehead with the woman.

Rema, who was now kneeling by the girl, silenced the feud: "Ray, go call an ambulance. And you," motioning to the woman, "you go get something warm to cover her with."

Reluctantly, the two combatants parted. Parker returned shortly to find the young woman still standing there on the verge of tears and shivering almost as much as the little girl shivered under the two large beach towels Rema had placed over the small torso.

The wind was rising again as Parker approached the woman. This time he spoke softly, "Where are the blankets?"

She turned to him. Her eyes narrowed. Her mouth twitched at the corners.

Rema, still kneeling, asked the obvious: "What blankets?"

"The five new blankets I stuffed inside there last night!" Parker pointed to the busted screen door.

The woman's mouth melded into a crooked smile as she looked Parker up and down. Her eyes widened. Those eyes . . . those eyes were very familiar. Those eyes were . . . hey, those were . . . *Her* eyes.

"I sold them this morning," she said dryly.

THE PETER PAN CHRONICLES

It ain't eve—nin'——Al-mos' mor-nin'—It ain't

eve-nin'—Al-mos' mor-nin'—and the Lord done filled my

heart with song, and I think I see the ris-ing Sun!

It ain't evenin'   Almos' mornin'
It ain't evenin'   Almos' mornin'
And the Lord done filled
   my heart with song,
And I think I see
   the rising Sun!

He was soaring again, flying and falling, arms spread, wind cold in his face. And there below him was Macy in the most unorthodox free-fall Parker had seen since—Who was it? What was that kid's name? "Ross," that's it, the only fatality in Parker's paratrooper training camp, either lost consciousness or—"Macy!!" Parker screamed against the wind as he dove toward her.

Her eyes were open behind the goggles. She stared at Parker for an instant, locked in terror, then she reached out and grabbed him around the neck. They plunged like the proverbial sack of alley apples, with Parker struggling to free himself.

She'd never jumped before. Parker was now certain of it. She'd lied. "Twelve jumps, my ass!" he shouted in her ear. "Why lie? I would have taught you!" he wanted to say, but she squeezed his neck so tightly he could barely catch his breath. She was taking him with her. No, she wouldn't let go. Not this time. "Hold me close," she seemed to whisper, just as she'd always done. "Closer."

It was Jamila's small arms squeezing his neck almost choking him, as Parker waded into deep water. "Not so tight!" Then suddenly the footing fell away and Parker went under. They both panicked. Jamila squeezed even tighter, choking him, drowning him. Parker instinctively dove as deep as he could. Jamila's instincts were equally good. She let go and struggled to the surface.

"Let go! Not now, Macy. Go and play!" Yeah, go and play with your parachute. It wasn't her parents' fault, though. No, it was those fingers. And some of the women didn't even have those Piaf fingers, but they still had the need.

"Ever have them times when you can't eat enough, drink enough?"

Too many had the need and "Doctor" Parker couldn't possibly make all the rounds. And besides, the cure that was demanded, "Deeper, please. Oh, yes, harder!", wasn't what was really required. That something was beyond the tactile, way beyond, but the touch did seem the closest thing to it this side of the veil. "Just hold me. Never let go," she whispered.

But like that of all doctors of the chronically or terminally ill, Parker's patience was thin, his anger quick. And he was rapidly running out of sky. If he simply pulled her ripcord, she'd take his head off when the air hit the chute. Instead he punched her between the shoulder blades to break her grip, pushed her to arm's length, and then pulled her cord. She was still grasping at his sleeve when the recoil whipped her skyward.

As he pulled his own cord, Parker knew it might already be too late. He was coming in too fast, heading for a stand of trees. . . .

There was an old photograph there among the leaves on the ground. A picture of Doris? It must have fallen from his pocket. What pocket? She seemed to be wearing that dress, a shirtwaist, the one she was wearing the last day.

What had she said? Something about lying being his job and how she could hardly expect it not to spill over on her.

Parker gazed at the faded image. Amazing. Even with the invention of photography, people still didn't understand the mystery of it. Shadow-catching, the Amer-Indians called it. Shadows of the young and now old. Shadows with apparent life though their casters be long dead. Shadows only.

Parker wanted to reach for the photo, but it was too far away and he had nothing with which to reach.

Parker had never noticed that there were so many women in his life. He thought he'd spent most of his time with men. Now somehow they were absent, perhaps confined to the treetops. But all the women were there, even Rema and Janet. Rema was playing hide-and-seek with him among the trees. At the same time she seemed oblivious to him, as she laughed and joked with the other women. One of the recurring jokes seemed to be Ray Parker. After prime-ribs-Rollins, Rema regarded Parker as a kind of junk-food binge. And, no, she wasn't above a binge every now and then. Strange how her laughter seemed to cry.

Janet's twin was there, or perhaps it was only that Parker had read her wrong from the start. He hadn't liked the old Janet. She was too much a function of her men. This Janet seemed different. She confronted Parker directly and told him that he hadn't injured her or Kweku but only himself. Her face revealed neither pity nor envy as she handed Parker a journal and drifted away. No, this was no longer dreamy-eyed Janet. What had he once said about such women?

"The male pragmatist and the female dreamer are high-tension oddities. And having effected that wholesale polarity shift, the whites are dangerous indeed!" It was in Sieber's book. Had Parker said that, or was it Rachael's editorializing? After all, in Rachael's hands, Sieber's dream of Parker's Forest sojourn had become the psychohistory of modern man.

---------- KWEKU'S ----------
JOURNAL

5 March 1973

The Gross-Mire Play
(A Fable For Willie and Ray)

Scene: A deserted street. Time: 5 A.M.

An old man clutches a faded picture ripped long ago from a magazine. His hands obscure most of it, as he holds it close to his breast. A young man approaches snickering: "Ah, dirty pictures! Let me see!"

The old man regards the young man with scorn for a moment and then turns his back on him. The young man persists, peering over the old man's hunched shoulders. The old man relents a bit, revealing a corner of the picture: there are a pair of eyes with the same lustful glint as that of the young man. The eyes seem to be peeping through some kind of foliage at what looks like the top of the moon, a kind of radiant silvery disc.

"Don't tell me," jokes the young man, leering and nudging the old man in the back, "it's the Devil eyeing the moon!"

"You see nothing," replies the old man, almost spitting the words. "It's only a mischievous boy eying the groom."

Before the young man, his mouth agape, can speak, the old man whirls about and thrusts the picture in the young man's face. The youth surveys the whole picture with gleeful intent: there are the eyes which now seem to be peering over tall grass. The "moon" is actually the top of the head of one of two birds. The bird the old man had called the "groom" appears indignant as he marches off in one direction, feathers flying. The groom is erect, obviously full of pride and determination, and the "lines of indignation" the artist has placed above his head make it appear radiant. On the other end of the picture and headed in the opposite direction is what appears to be the "bride." She, too, is radiant, but with "lines of apprehension." She is bent forward, almost tearful. Her gait is wider, making her appear to move more swiftly than the groom. She too moves in a flurry of flying feathers. The area which both birds are vacating is occupied by an object more radiant than either of them. It is a tiny, silvery egg nestled in a clump of twigs.

"What do you see?" asks the old man.

"Well," says the young man in full bravado, "they just had a brat and already they've busted up! You see it all the time!"

"You see nothing," says the old man, almost in a whisper, as he begins to withdraw the picture.

"Now wait a minute," rails the young man, grabbing the old man by both wrists so that the picture remains before him, "let me look again."

"What of the boy?" asks the old man.

The young man, loosening his grip: "Why, he mocks them, the silly birds. Look, he's laughing at them!"

"As you mock me? Look again, for you see nothing."

Obviously agitated, the young man suggests that perhaps the boy has frightened the birds, and that they flee at his coming.

"Do you think that they would *both* desert the egg?"

"How the hell should I know?" shouts the young man, almost in rage.

"You see nothing," begins the old man. "These are Gross-mire birds. Once they mate they are partners for life. From this picture, one might say this pair is capable of mating maybe three or four more times in their life together. Yet, each year an egg is laid these birds must perform a ceremony of reaffirmation. First, they wait for a breeze. Then they both must ruffle their feathers and each must catch one feather of the other in its beak before that feather touches the ground or is swept by the breeze to far-off stream or treetop. These two feathers are the first to be placed in the nest. If under any circumstance either bird fails to catch one feather of the other, the two birds can never mate again. They must live out their lives in barrenness."

The young man is by this time bored to distraction. Releasing the old man's wrists, he tries to leave. But the old man continues: "In this picture the ceremony has just begun as the boy blunders on the scene. The groom in his masculine pride *knows* he can catch the feather, place it in the nest, and pluck out the eyes of the intruder in one swoop. The bride more fully grasps the enormity of the danger involved in this encounter. She senses the *mindlessness* of an intruding creature who knows not of the Law.

"Will she go for the feather or will she spring to the defense of her family? 'What a decision!' you say. But there are no decisions for animals. She will simply *yield* to that force which drives her most relentlessly either to preserve life now or to preserve the possibility of future life."

With that the old man releases the picture, which, caught in the wind, sails past the young man's ear. In a vain attempt to grab it, the young man succeeds only in slapping himself in the face. Embarrassed by his own clumsiness, he turns back to vilify the old man, only to find that he is not there. Look as he might, the young man sees nothing.

THIRTY-THREE

Of course, there are those who say that there never was an explosion and that Raynard Parker still lies cancer-ridden and thoroughly thorazined in that West German prison hospital. Others suspect that he died back in '74 with Tommy Rollins or that the two were one and the same, that "Kweku" was just another one of Ray's aliases.

A lot of people believe that Margaret Gruber had a vision and probably became a healer. But then, many dispute that.

And the junkie stories abound. But no one tells a better one than Jerome, Rema's younger son. He says that there was this one morning out in the woods behind the projects when he and his two partners, Ricardo and Fred, had just finished shooting up and were into a giggling nod when this naked man came barreling into them, knocking everybody every which way, but mostly down.

"Well, that was some good shit, man, I wants to tell you. I didn't even mind gittin' knocked down. And might not had even remembered it if my mama hadn't showed up just then with the biggest knife I done ever seen. Now, she done already said she gonna kill me if she catch me coppin' another nod. So I figure I'm dead. And I wants to tell you I was so fucked up I didn't even give a shit. Fact is, I looks over at the naked mothafucka to say goodbye and there he is struggling to get up with this gun in his hand and it's pointin' dead at my nose. Well, Ricardo says I jus' started laughin' then. I don't remember, gun or knife didn't make no difference to me, that was some good shit, man! Fred said he thought my moms was gonna kill all of us, so he drags ass outta there. But Ricardo says what my moms did was grab the gun barrel in one hand and slice that mothafucka's hand off with the other. And as she snatched the gun away that hand went sailin' through the air. Ricardo says I was laughin' the whole time until that hand hit me dead in the mouth. Then I puked my guts out. I don't remember nothin' after that except that was some good shit, man, I wants to tell you!"

Then there are those who swear they saw Parker on TV among the American hostages during that recent embassy takeover. Janet Fields was so certain it was Ray that she sent Kweku's journal to Parker there.

They say Parker's captors were more than happy to pass the journal along once they had scanned its contents. And some report that it was this journal that Parker flung at them on the morning of his breakdown. All of this, however, is impossible to confirm.

Or as Willie might say: "These days, so and not so don't make much difference at all. Once the bones are scattered, we free to dream another dream, soar where we will on gross-mire wings."

That's "gossamer," Willie, "gossamer."

EPILOGUE

Rema hit her stride at the piano as an old fellow way in the back—could have been anybody, nobody, just somebody in off the streets to beat the cold—this old guy falls right in with it, dead on the bass part. Didn't quite have the words yet, but he'd pick 'em up the next time 'round:

>   Hitainevenin   Halmosmornin
>   Hitainevenin   Halmosmornin

The strength of his voice brought Rema's head up from the keys. As their eyes met, they exchanged a nod and she lined it out for him.

PS
3556
.R88
P48
1989

PS
3556
.R88
P48
1989